DANCE OF LIFE

Dance of Life

MARGOT GRIFFIN
ILLUSTRATED BY P. JOHN BURDEN

Fitzhenry & Whiteside

Text copyright © 2005 by Margot Griffin.
Illustration copyright © 2005 by P. John Burden.

Published in Canada by Fitzhenry & Whiteside, 195 Allstate Parkway,
Markham, Ontario L3R 4T8

Published in the United States by Fitzhenry & Whiteside,
121 Harvard Avenue, Suite 2, Allston, Massachusetts 02134

www.fitzhenry.ca   **godwit@fitzhenry.ca**

10 9 8 7 6 5 4 3 2 1

Library and Archives Canada Cataloguing in Publication

Griffin, Margot
     The dance of life / Margot Griffin; illustrations by P. John Burden.
(A Meggy tale)

ISBN 1-55005-125-3

     I. Burden, P. John, 1943- II. Title. III. Series: Griffin, Margot. Meggy tale.
PS8563.R5352D29 2004   jC813'.6   C2004-903787-0

**U.S. Publisher Cataloging-in-Publication Data
(Library of Congress Standards)**

Griffin, Margot.
     The dance of life / Margot Griffin; illustration by P. John Burden.—1st ed.
[190] p. : ill.; cm. (A Meggy tale)
Summary: When a mine accident incapacitates her Da, Meggy must take to the
roads as County Kerry's first Dance Mistress to save her family from eviction.
ISBN 1-55005-125-3 (pbk.)
1. Teenagers—Fiction—Juvenile literature. 2. Ireland (County Kerry)—
Juvenile fiction. 3. Dance—Juvenile fiction.
I. Burden, P. John. II. Griffin, Margot. Maggy tales. III. Title.
[Fic] dc22   PZ7.G754456Da   2004

Fitzhenry & Whiteside acknowledges with thanks the Canada Council for the Arts, the
Government of Canada through the Book Publishing Industry Development Program
(BPIDP), and the Ontario Arts Council for their support of our publishing program.

Design: Fortunato Design Inc.
Printed and bound in Canada

As with Meggy's family, "Disaster Came a-Knockin'" at our door and left "A Monster of an Illness." Each day I must outdance it. Thankfully I am not alone. My dear family Phil, Nicole, Robbie and Gwodzie are devoted dance partners.

I am blessed with exceptional physicians, Dr. J. Sangster and Dr. R. Feldman. With knowledge and compassion they keep me on life's dance floor, leading on when others would have given up. It is because you continue to try that I continue to hope.

Words cannot express the difference my beloved nurse, Toula Gerace, makes in my life. With wisdom and compassion, she coaches me. She encourages me to analyze my steps, so that I may continue to find new ways to enjoy the dance.

It is because of your loving acceptance that I can admit I am afraid.

Rosemarie and Roxanne, bring daily comfort to my soul as well as my body. Because of you I feel ready for the dance of the day that awaits me.

Thank you, dance partners, one and all. Because of you, I keep on dancing.

CONTENTS

FOREWORD

What do you think your life will be like at thirteen or fourteen? Meggy MacGillycuddy of County Kerry, Ireland, is now fourteen years old. At twelve, most girls of her time (the mid-1700s) would be well finished with school.

But not Meggy—in fact, her vigilance as their hiding school's lookout made it possible for her brother Dan and the other little ones to escape capture by the English soldiers.

Did she run home to Mam when the others were safe? No, she turned back to save the wounded Master Cleary. Would you be brave enough to stay behind, alone, to rescue your favorite teacher from soldiers?

Have you thought about becoming a teacher someday? At thirteen, when other girls her age were getting married, Meggy and her best friend Fiona were searching for a new hiding school location. And then, just when they started to enjoy teaching their classes in the crystal cave, a Red Witch threatens their safety. Meggy led the children in coming up with a secret plan to trap the traitor and escape from the soldiers.

Have you ever faced the fear of losing a parent or becoming homeless? A terrible mining accident threatens her father's life and leaves him unable to work. Meggy must travel, in disguise, through the night-dark roads of Kerry trying to earn enough money to save her family from losing their home.

In this, the last tale of her trilogy, will Meggy survive *The Dance of Life*?

1

❖❖

DISASTER COMES A-KNOCKIN'

Meggy knew from the loud pounding at their door that something was wrong.

She knew it was the worst kind of wrong when, after listening to the man at the door, Mam grabbed her shawl and her healing basket and left.

In the bed beside her, Dan stirred and reached out for warmth of his mother. When he realized her spot was empty he asked his sister sleepily, "Where's Mam?"

Not knowing just what to say Meggy answered, "She and her healin' basket are needed at the mine."

Dan sat right up, "But Meggy, she left without kissin' me. Mam never leaves without kissin' us goodbye."

Leaning over she gave her brother a quick hug and said,

"Dan, I know no more of why Mam left so quickly." In one quick movement she rolled over and slid out of their settle bed. Tugging on her little brother's feet she added, "But I do know that there is work to be doin'. I'll make you breakfast if you go to the peat pile and carry in all that is there." It wasn't that they wouldn't need peat for the fire. But Meggy also needed a few minutes alone to try to stop the fearsome images that kept racing through her mind. She sat down and tried to take some deep breaths, tried to blow the fear away.

By the time Dan came in, staggering under the weight of his last load, she had his breakfast ready. While he ate she stood on tiptoe, blindly reaching into the cupboard high up beside the chimney. Pulling out rolled strips of white cloth she remembered how she had last used them to bind her bosom so no soldier would guess she was old enough to be teaching.

For so long now, Meggy and the others had focused only on the soldiers and informers as their enemies. They had forgotten how one wrong move, one inexplicable act of nature could, in a single second, change a good man's life forever.

His breakfast gobbled Dan asked, "When is Mam coming home? Will she be here to make me dinner?"

Trying to keep him too busy to ask more questions she said, "Dan, go to the McSorley's. Tell them about the miner comin' to our door. Ask Roddy to come back with you and bring some bogwood. The two of you can chop it up for kindlin'."

"Meggy, we've already got kindlin' out back," complained Dan.

Putting her brother's cap on his red curls, Meggy said, "No more blatherin', Dan. Off you go. Maybe Roddy will ride ye back on his shoulders."

Meggy stood alone, wishing her best friend Fiona was there. "I know she would say, 'Let us pray.'" Meggy dropped to her knees and prayed for Da's safe return. Then needing to be busy she scrubbed their table, the table her da had built, as if she could wash her troubles away.

Dan's shouting made her jump. "Roddy, don't put me down yet. Someone is comin'. It looks like the parade we made when we carried Fancy Feet's body to the graveyard."

When she heard Dan say the word "body", Meggy's knees buckled. When her strength returned she moved to the door. Looking down the path, she could see nothing. "Dan, you're not teasin' me, are ye? This is no time for one of your wild tales."

Roddy had taken a few more steps along the path. He said, "Meggy, step up here. You'll see them comin' up over the rise." Before she could take that step, Roddy's da came into view leading four men, carrying a fifth on a makeshift stretcher. Meggy saw her mam by the stretcher, never once taking her eyes off the man lying there.

"No, it's not! It can't be!" thought Meggy, not wanting to believe what her mind was telling her. By the time she could make her fear-frozen feet move, the Kerry rain was falling on the miners' faces, making it hard tell whether the streaks that washed white through the mine-dust were caused by rain or tears.

◆

3

Meggy hoped against hope. "Many a time, Mam has been called on to tend a sorely injured man. Many a time she has brought one here to watch over him."

When the poor man began coughing, struggling for every breath, her mother ordered, "Put the stretcher down. Sit him up. We must help him breathe!"

It was then that Meggy saw the face, the features no amount of dirt or blood could hide. She tried to call out to her father, but fear had completely throttled her. She would have fallen, if Roddy had not put one long arm around her to pull her to him. It was Dan who called out in disbelief, "Meggy, it's not Da, is it? Please tell me it's not our da!"

Her little brother's need for her snapped Meggy out of her shock enough to reach out to hold his hand. Looking up at him, still on his perch upon Roddy's shoulders, Meggy said, "Yes, Dan. It is our da, and our mam too. Aren't we the lucky ones to have a mother who knows more about healin' than anyone else in the village of Copperkin?" Meggy saw her words drew Dan's attention away from their sorely injured father, so she kept talking. "Think of all the other fathers and brothers that have been brought here for Mam to tend. Think of all of them, as good as new now."

"Mam will make Da better, won't she Meggy?" said Dan with hope in his voice.

Meggy had to struggle to speak over the lump in her throat, "Mam will give Da the best care that any County Kerry miner ever received. And we'll help too."

◆

Thumping sounds drew Meggy's and Danny's eyes back to their father. They winced in unison as their mother pounded his back. Shocked, Danny asked, "Meggy, why is Mam hittin' Da like that?"

She could barely watch as her mother and then a miner pounded hard on her poor father's back. Just when Meggy was about to answer Dan, their father coughed so hard it seemed as if his innards might come up. Even though she felt the pain of the pounding in her own ribs Meggy knew it was good for Da to get as much minedust out as possible.

When he stopped coughing, the men lay him gently back down and, picking the stretcher up, they hurried past the three statue-still children. After lifting him onto the McGillycuddy's table, their only table, the one Mac himself had built, they stepped back.

Mam said, "Meggy, I'll be needin' strong soap, boilin' water and some clean white rags."

"It is all ready for ye, Mam," said Meggy, glad to have done the right thing.

Putting her arm around her daughter, Mrs. MacGillycuddy spoke to her son, "Dan, we'll be needin' all the peat from out back and perhaps even more."

"I did it already," said Dan proudly. "And I'm just goin' to bring in the kindlin' Roddy is choppin' for us."

"You've done well, me darlins. What would I ever do without ye?" asked Mam, as she drew her children to her for an all-too-short hug.

Passing the rolls of cloth to her mother, Meggy said, "Just tell me what to do."

Her mother's heart filled, half with sorrow that her daughter had needed to grow up so fast and half with gratitude for the brave, helpful young woman she was becoming.

"Alright, Meggy, we'll do this together. You take care of those dreadful gashes on your da's head. I'll take off his shirt and check for wounds there."

Meggy studied her father's battered face, trying to decide where to start. Although he lay there stone-still, she began talking to him. "I must be cleanin' the blood and dirt from your wounds. I'll do me best not to hurt ye, Da." She watched for a response. His eyes remained closed, his lips motionless.

"I think it might be best to be gettin' the worst over first," said Meggy, dampening the hair on his brow, hair that was once raven-black like hers. But now it was streaked with gray even when it wasn't filled with mine dirt. She winced as she pulled blood-glued strands of hair out of the deep, gaping gash on his forehead.

"Stop! Stop! Da is dead ! No man alive could lie there and let you do that to him," cried Dan. "Da is dead!"

Dan had been standing still and forgotten, watching what no small boy should ever have to see. Meggy pulled him to her. "Dan, put your ear by Da's chest. Do you hear those rattly wheezes? That's him workin' hard to breath. As long as Da is breathin', he's alive."

◆

Mam reached over their father's death-still body to touch her son's tear-streaked cheek. "Dan, it's a blessin' your da can't feel the pain." Then she returned to the difficult task of pulling up her husband's shirt without injuring him further.

Strong as she was trying to be, their mam could not hold back a gasp of horror. There on Da's chest was the deep, bruise-darkened outline of one of the heavy beams that were supposed to keep the mine's tunnels from collapsing.

She turned to the miners, hovering around their table like four rugged angels watching over their foreman, their friend. "You'd best be tellin' me what happened."

With a deep sigh, a miner with a huge bloody bump on his head began, "A grand band of copper was found in the newest tunnel yesterday…"

Another man, sitting on a stool because of the boulder-sized bruising on his legs, broke in: "Mac investigated, an' he found the lake seepin' through. He declared it off limits for our crew."

The next miner was trembling from his toes up. "Word of the new find got to the landlord. First thing this mornin', Lord Black was waitin' for us. He offered two months free rent to the miner who would work the tunnel and bring him more. Always more…"

With a deep shuddering breath this teller stopped his telling. As it had taken all of them to carry Mac home, it was now taking the four of them to tell his terrible tale.

"After His Lordship left, Mac again banned all of us from

steppin' foot into that tunnel. But it wasn't long before he got word that young Finbar O'Mara had boldly declared, 'No one will stop me from winnin' that free rent. Nell and I have our first babe comin'. It's time I was providin' me family with a home of our own.'"

"When your man heard of Finbar's plans he went after him—alone, not allowin' us to go with him. We didn't want to disobey Mac…"

"But we four went as far as the mouth of the tunnel, just in case he needed us."

"No sooner did we get there than we heard a crash, far louder than thunder. We had only time to turn our backs and put our hands over our heads. Rocks came beatin' down upon us, as if hurled by an angry giant. When it stopped we turned around…"

"What once had been the tunnel opening was now a huge slate fall, much taller than ourselves. At the top was a small hole. We scrambled up and peered in by the light of our candles. All we saw was a total darkness of rocks. We called 'Mac! Finbar! Are ye there?' until we could call no more."

"Never have we dug out a slate fall so fast. When the hole was big enough we slid headfirst into the darkness. Then we began to crawl over the broken rock, not wantin' to cause another fall. We turned our candles to each corner. All we saw was a hundred different shades of black and gray."

"We were movin' on to the fourth corner, when I saw

somethin'. There it was—a candle—not lit but still a spot of pale in all that dark. We crawled to the candle and saw the big hand below it. It had to be Mac. He has the biggest hands of us all. We tugged at the hand—we squeezed it—nothin'."

"The worst came when we tore the stones off Mac's face. All of us were hopin' for one of his slow smiles or quick winks. There was nothin', not even a whisper of a breath. We threw off the rocks still coverin' him, still no change. But there it was, that huge beam layin' right across his chest, crushin' the very breath out of him."

"Usually it takes eight of us to move one of those beams. But there was Mac, with only us to help him. We knew we would never lift it so we pushed and shoved big rocks under each end, raisin' it higher and higher. Finally we had the space we needed. Usin' every last bit of strength we had, we pulled Mac out. The moment that beam was off his chest, he started breathin', not talkin', not movin', but at least a raspy kind of breathin'."

A big sigh of relief moved round the table. The men started making leaving motions but Vera stopped them, "What about Finbar? You've not told us about Fin."

The men dropped their heads and looked at their boots. The only sound in the cottage was Da's ragged wheezing.

She asked again, "What about Fin?"

The man with the bump on his head was the first to look up. Glancing at Meggy and then Dan, he asked, "Are ye sure you want me to be tellin' ye now?"

◆

10

"Tell us," she said.

With his voice a-quiver, the miner said, "When I went to shove rocks under the far end of the beam, I saw him. There was not a mark on him. His face was as handsome as the day he took Nell to be his bride. Fin might have been lyin' there waitin' for her to kiss him good-mornin'. Except for his neck…"

A cry like that of a newborn kitten escaped Meggy's throat. Dan's little shoulders shook as he buried his face in her skirt. Their mother moved around the table to pull them to her.

The whole, terrible table now told, one of the miners said, "If you're no longer needin' us, Vera, we'll be goin' along now. Our women will soon be here to help ye. Would you like me to be takin' young Dan home with me?"

Dan hated seeing his father like this, but he was more afraid of never seeing him alive again. So he shook his head no when his mother looked into his face. "'Tis kind of you to ask," she said. "Perhaps Meggy will bring him along later."

Meggy knew she was not going anywhere. Holding her father's big hand in hers she silently promised, "Da, I won't be leavin' ye. You're always tellin' me that you can feel life surgin' round me when I dance. Feel it now, Da. Feel it surge from me to you, so you may live to see me dance again."

2

❖

A MONSTER OF AN ILLNESS

For the next five days Meggy's family fell into a pattern of caring, watching, and waiting. All movement centered around their father, lying in what seemed to be a forever kind of sleep.

The eyes of mother, daughter, and son turned in an unspoken schedule to the man on the bed, checking and hoping. Dan wanted things to be as they used to be. He would sit crosslegged on the bed telling his father about his adventures. Then he would lean in nose to nose so he could be sure to see the smallest change. He was sure that his tale about a baby dragon would earn a response. But there was not even the hint of a smile. Disappointed, Dan turned to get down. A flash of color stopped him. What he saw set him bouncing on the bed and shouting, "Da's awake! Da's awake!"

❖

All that Meggy could manage at seeing her da's blue-of-the-lake eyes staring at her was, "Oh Da, dear Da."

Mam gently settled Dan down and then sat on the bed. Taking her husband's hands in her own she said, "Welcome back, me darlin' Mac."

Her father looked so puzzled, Meggy said, "There was a terrible mine accident."

"And you've been asleep for five whole days," added Dan.

When their da said nothing Mam asked, "Can you hear us, Mac?"

Then Meggy took a turn, "Can you talk? Can you call me your darlin' Meggy?"

He tried but could only utter a terrible garble of harsh sounds and unintelligibilities. When he made a writing motion with his hand, Mam brought their only pen and Meggy gave him the back page of her precious Robin Hood book. The three words her father wrote there would forever cause her pain.

WHO ARE YOU?

* * *

The villagers were amazed that Mac MacGillycuddy had cheated death despite being buried alive; that he could breathe again after the huge beam left its mark permanently on his chest; that he was able to think at all after the bashing his head took.

◆

Mac's family paid no heed to what was being said. They were far too busy trying to take care of him. Meggy had no time for her friends, not even her best friend. When Fiona arrived with a pie, Mam sent Meggy out. "I know you're needin' Fiona more than ever, love. Have a wee visit on the bench by the door and you'll be close if we need ye."

Fiona said not a word. She held her best friend's hands and looked searchingly into her eyes. Meggy, who had taken no time for her own feelings, could not keep them from tumbling out now. "Oh Fiona, we spend every wakin' minute carin' for Da. But it seems as if he will never be well again."

Fiona gently pulled her friend's head onto her own thin shoulder. When the tears slowed she reached into her pocket and pulled out a handful of scrap paper. "These are for your da. We heard he could write a bit. Do his messages help him connect with you?"

"How I wish that were true! His first message broke our hearts. He asked, 'Who are you?' Me own father doesn't even know me! I hope every message will say something wonderful like, 'I love ye, Meggy.' But mostly they are a word or two for something he needs, like water.

"Often he just points. If we don't understand or can't read his writin' he gets so frustrated his whole body stiffens and his face turns purple. I'm ashamed I feel impatient some-times." Meggy fell into a silence of sighs. Fiona patted her comfortingly.

◆

Ready to go on, Meggy said, "Takin' care of Da is not easy. He has terrible headaches and not even Mam's herbs help him. When we have to thump his back hard, again and again, he looks at us as if we are deliberately tryin' to hurt him."

Mam called to her from inside, "Can you give me just a moment, Meggy, an' help Dan and me to get Da in his chair?"

Roddy and Mr. McSorley had built him a heavy chair with a high back. Because their father fought them, putting him into it was a job that took all three of them and sometimes even a neighbor, too. Meggy saw the sorrow and sympathy in her best friend's face and could accept it from her, only her.

Fiona rose with Meggy, ready to help her friend with even this most difficult task.

Coming inside, they saw Dan shrinking back. "Mam, Mam—do we have to tie Da in his chair today?" Taking one look at the pain in her mother's face, Meggy answered her brother.

"Dan, you know Da won't stay in bed. He wants to sit up, but he's too dizzy. Just two days ago he fell and broke open ten of the stitches Mam sewed up his forehead with. He might never get better if he falls and hurts his head again."

That day, making Da safe in his chair went surprisingly well. Fiona knelt in front of him and in her soft voice shared the beauty of her walk through the fall woods. Before she finished her lovely tale, they were done tying their knots in the back, and their father was nodding off. All of the MacGillycuddys were grateful for her visit.

◆

Fiona continued to show up to help. She was there, one month later, to cheer with Meggy and Dan when their father no longer needed to be tied in his chair. When he began to eat soft foods by himself, the MacGillycuddys' meal times became more normal. They could once again sit around the table, with Da in his proper place at the head. When he began to take a trembling step or two on his own, their hopes for his independence grew.

Every one of the miners had been to the MacGillycuddys' carryin' what food they could spare. Each had stood in front of their foreman, the man they most respected and asked, "How are ye doin', Mac?" Each received the same silent answer. Each felt a finger of fear travel up their spines. They tried hard not see a dismal future for Mac's family.

Danny kept trying to make things the way they used to be. He sat on a stool next to his brooding father. Holding out a piece of wood and a small whittling knife he said, "Da, now that you are home all day you can finish teachin' me how to carve me wee lamb."

Wary of the knife, Meggy stood up. But her mother's eyes asked her to just watch—to trust.

To her surprise, Da took the knife and the wood that already had four tiny lamb legs carved out of it. He made a curved cut that Dan knew was the lamb's back. Then the knife fell from his father's hands, clattering to the floor. In frustration Da threw the lamb after it. He looked at his son with such anger in his face that Dan fell backwards off his stool. Once on the floor he bravely reached out and picked up the lamb. But one little leg had broken off and now lay where Dan dare not go—between his father's big feet. In one graceful dancer's move Meggy swooped down and retrieved the bit of wood.

When she handed it to Dan he whispered, "Da doesn't love me anymore."

"Ah, Dan, Da still loves you and Mam and me too. It's just the terrible monster of his illness," Meggy comforted him, with words she was not sure she believed herself.

She grieved the loss of the father she used to have, the one replaced by this grim stranger in the chair. Dan, who had always been able to make his father laugh, grew quieter and quieter. And Mam, once tall and straight, seemed to grow more stooped each day. Sometimes, after one of Da's raging nightmares had woken them all, Meggy heard her mother's muffled sobs as she cried herself back to sleep. But never once did she see her shed a tear in front of herself, Dan or Da.

Now Mam called her children to her. "I know your da is hard on ye. But he's still your father. He is not himself—yet. We must protect him, in all ways, just like he did for us."

Her children took her hands and promised, "Yes, Mam."

Their mother was grateful to have some good news to share, "Mr. McSorley has arranged for your father's friends to come and carry him to the pub. It will be good for him to get out with the men. But he won't be goin' anywhere if we don't get him dressed."

◆

This was a process none of the MacGillycuddys enjoyed. Da hated to have his young son pull on his boots, his daughter to wash his face, and the worst indignity of all—his wife to haul his trousers up. Just the moment they were done, his cronies came through the door singing at the top of their lungs.

Meggy blessed the men. She had been afraid Da might fall if the ride was too rowdy. But they were gently lifting him and his chair up in small stages. They cheered for him with each lift. "Hurrah, hurrah, hurrah for Mac."

Their cheers gave her father his first smile since the accident. Dan was hopping and skipping behind the procession, doing his own little tag-along jig. Before he got away with the men, Mam tugged him back gently by the collar. As they stood in the doorway waving goodbye, Meggy put her arm around her mother. It was the first time all four MacGillycuddys had been happy in weeks.

Wanting to keep her brother smiling, Meggy held out the little bit of wood and said, "Look Dan, if you pat some coal-dust on his face, he'll look just like Office Lamb from our Crankanny school. Let's go into the woods before the sun sets and see if we can find a bit of sap to mend his leg."

It took them only a few minutes to find a tiny, almost solid golden drop of sap. Picking it off the bark they took turns rolling it in their fingers. Finally it was soft enough to glue the little lamb's leg back on. Dan gave her a grateful smile, but it didn't reach his eyes. Meggy couldn't help but wish there was a glue for mending broken hearts.

◆

That night all four MacGillycuddys slept snugly together again. Da's visit to the pub gave him his first nightmare-free sleep. They woke the next day, warm, cozy and as a family. Da was last to open his eyes. When he did, something new was in them. Dan discovered the change as he crawled up beside his father's head, to peer right into his eyes, "You know me now, Da, don't ye? You really know me."

As Da met Mam's and Meggy's eyes, the looks of recognition were so strong there was no need for words. They joined Dan on the bed and laughed and hugged and kissed, like Meggy had been afraid they never would again.

Trying to keep the happiness going, Meggy and her mother decided that Da would enjoy sitting out front, in the shade of the old oak. Mam said, "It is so beautiful out here, with the sun turnin' the leaves gold. I wish I could just sit awhile meself." Each grabbing one arm, they dragged Da's heavy chair outside.

Returning, they found him frantically searching the scrap-paper pile. "What do you need?" asked Mam. Da angrily mimed the action of writing.

Meggy handed him the pen. Then she watched over his shoulder in horror as he attacked the paper.

You two—shame me—sit me out front—when good men work—all stare—whisper—lazy mac macgillycuddy.

*NO OUT—STAY INSIDE—away from stare—*He dragged the pen so viciously across the paper that it made a ragged hole where the "s" of *stares* would have been. Staggering through the door he took hold of his chair.

◆

19

Taking the other arm, Meggy said, "I'll help ye, Da."

Shaking his head *no*, he yanked the heavy chair out of her hand. He spent several minutes bumping and crashing it back inside. Collapsing into it, he fell asleep.

Turning away from him, Meggy and Mam saw Dan standing there. Having just returned from the privy, he had witnessed his father's angry actions.

Meggy spoke first, "Where did our real da go? He was with us earlier—but now that angry, angry man is back. Will Da ever be his real self again?"

Putting her arm around her heartsick daughter, Mam gave the only honest answer she knew, "We don't know. He might and he might not."

Dan spoke angrily to them, "Don't say he might not! I know Da won't be like this forever! You should too! When they brought him home, he couldn't even wake up. Then he couldn't sit up, without bein' tied in his chair. Everytime he tried to stand he fell down. Last night he didn't have one nightmare! This morning he knew us! HOW CAN YOU SAY HE MIGHT NOT GET BETTER? HE IS GETTIN' BETTER EVERY DAY!"

Meggy thought a moment and then said, "Mam, Dan is right. When Da first came home, lookin' into his eyes was like lookin' into an abandoned mine shaft with no life left in it. This mornin', there was life and maybe even love there."

Pulling her children to her, Mam said, "I hope you're right. I hope your da will recover quickly." Of the four of them, only she knew the disasters that could befall their family if he didn't. As if on cue, there was a loud pounding at the door. Remembering the last pounding, each MacGillycuddy felt fear touch them. Meggy took a step forward and opened it.

There, smirking and holding a piece of rolled-up paper in one hand, stood Seamus Fox, the landlord's man. He had turned his back on his family and his fellow Irish by doing Lord Black's dirty work.

"Good day, Mrs. MacGillycuddy and to your lovely daughter too," he said, so busy leering at Meggy that he didn't notice Dan at all. "And aren't you the lucky family to be receivin' a personal letter from His Lordship."

Snatching the message Meggy said, "What kind of message from His Lordship could be good for us? Why, this is not good luck at all! It is an eviction notice."

Seamus took another step toward her. He was so close she could smell the stench of the green mold growing on his teeth. "You and yours should be grateful, Miss Meggy. If not for His Lordship's generosity, I would be evicting your family *today*. You are now one month behind on your rent."

If Fox wasn't so blinded by his own arrogance, he would have seen the twin flames of anger flare up in her green eyes and the rage rising red in her cheeks. He might not then have made his poorly timed offer. "But my lovely Meggy, if you agree to go to Lover's Cove with me tonight, I might be able to speak to His Lordship on your behalf."

◆

Meggy exploded in a volley of words, "I wouldn't consider even walkin' to the privy with ye! If not for your Lordship's greediness, Finbar O'Mara's babe would not be born fatherless! My father would still be earnin' our rent money, workin' in the dangerous conditions your Lordship allows at the mine. Instead me dear da sits here, trapped in a body that doesn't work for him. All because His Greediness wanted more, always more!"

"Yeah, more! Always more!" echoed Dan, sticking his tongue out at Seamus.

Fox paid no more attention to Dan than he would to an annoying fly. Raising his prissy eyebrows and looking down his pimpled nose at her, he announced in his fake English accent, "Miss Meggy, one day you will wish you had accepted my offer. It is dangerous for you to speak of His Lordship in such a disrespectful way. Someone might inform him of your traitorous words. Milord is generously allowing you to stay until Christmas Day. If you cannot pay *all* your rent then, it will be my pleasure to put the four of you out in the snow!"

Mam knew that angering this weasel of a man and his master Lord Black could result only in further disaster for her family. Stepping in front of Meggy and Dan, she said, "Thank you for deliverin' the notice, Seamus. Please tell Lord Black my family appreciates his generosity in extendin' our rent-due date. Word has it that His Lordship is sufferin' with the gout again. Please give him this sachet of soakin' powders as a token of our appreciation. Tell him I hope they'll be easin' his pain." Feeling the indignation of her children behind her, she closed the door.

Glancing over at her husband, Vera was grateful he was sleeping and had not witnessed that degrading scene. Explaining her actions to her angry children would be hard enough. First checking that the awful man was gone, she pushed them back out front. Tugging angrily on her skirt Dan demanded, "Mam, how could ye say thank ye to that awful man? Da would have sent him away before he even said, 'Good day.'"

"Dan, I'm sorry you don't agree with me actions. But I'm doin' the best I can to take care of our family till your da can again," explained Mam kindly but firmly.

Meggy too, was shocked. Stooping so low as to send a gift to the man who planned to evict them was not something a proud MacGillycuddy should ever do. But, noticing her mother's shaking hands, she realized what huge responsibilites she was shouldering. Taking one of her mam's hands into her own cold one and holding her brother's sweaty one in the other, she said, "Mam, I understand how hard it must have been for you to do what you did. Dan, if Mam had been as angry with Seamus as we were, we might all be out in the street right now, with no home to sleep in tonight. Mam, we'll stand by ye and support your decisions, won't we, Dan?"

Blinking back his tears, her little brother nodded *yes*.

◆

"But Mam, how will we keep from losin' our cottage?" worried Meggy, with fear for the future rising in her throat. "Without bein' able to speak or keep his balance, Da can't go back to the mine."

"Don't fret, Meggy. I've been doin' some thinkin'," said Mam, trying to reassure her children, despite her own dark thoughts. "They've been workin' short-handed at the pub, since Deirdre was fired for being a traitor. I'm goin' tomorrow to ask for the job."

Dan said, "I'll go with you and whistle for coins at the back door."

"Good thinkin', Dan. But you will be accompanyin' me, not Mam," said Meggy. "Mam, you can't be leavin' Da. He needs your healin' skills. I'll go see about that job. I should have thought of it sooner."

"Meggy, I thought you might be plannin' another hedge school, but were waitin' till your da didn't need so much help," said Mam.

"I love teachin' the little ones. But it is too dangerous to start another school now, with the soldiers still angry about not finding the last one," said Meggy. "So, I'm off to get me that job. I wonder if I can earn extra coins by carrying drinks and dancing at the same time?" With a fancy step or two she was off to the pub.

It took only one hopeful step inside to destroy Meggy's dreams of a paying job. Another young woman, with an apron tied about her rounding belly, was serving drinks.

One glance at the other's face sent Meggy's heart tugging in two directions. She wished she had gotten to the pub job first, but immediately was ashamed. For the new barmaid was Nell.

"She's only three years older than me and her shoulders are already hunched over," Meggy thought. "It's as if the weight of the slate fall is pushin' her down, like it crushed the life out of her darlin' Fin." Nell had spent a month at the entrance to the mine, day after day keening and calling out, "Fin, Fin—we're waitin' for ye, Fin." She had not believed she would never see her husband again. Then the tunnel had collapsed a second time, claiming his young body forever.

Meggy was truly glad Nell had returned to the living enough to be able to work to support herself and the babe to come. Still, as she ran outside, her own heart ached with worry.

"What will happen to me family? Will we be homeless come Christmas?"

3

❖

ḣOPE

Roddy been at the pub when the smarmy Seamus Fox stopped by to put the fear of the landlord into them all by describing his delivery of the MacGillycuddys' eviction notice. Roddy had felt every man there clench his fists and grit his teeth. He knew they would have liked nothing more than to have thrown Fox into the dark of the lake where there was no swimming back. Unfortunately since all but he and his father, the pubkeep, worked at the landlord's mine, they couldn't risk losing their own jobs and leaving their families homeless too.

Leaving in disgust, he just missed Meggy and the disappointment that awaited her. Roddy had been sweet on Meggy since their Stoney Book hiding school, despite the fact that she called him "a useless waste of good Irish skin and bones," her eyes sparking as she spurned him. So he relished any errand that took him to the MacGillycuddys'.

Today he had a message to deliver, and on the way, Roddy thought about the times he had visited the since the accident. After he witnessed Meggy and her mam struggling to get Mac out of bed and into his chair he stopped by often to lend his strong arms to the job. Because Roddy cared for Meggy, he saw her pain as she watched her mam's hand shake while feeding Da as if he were a helpless babe. She saw Dan jump joyfully into bed with their father, only to see his little face crumple as their father pushed him away. Roddy had seen Meggy lay a calming hand on her mam's shoulder or tease Dan out of his troubles. But not once did he see her add her own sorrows to those that escaped in sighs from her mother and in bursts of temper from her brother.

Now, he found Meggy sitting where her worries had overtaken her: collapsed and crying behind the well. The well's stony wall gave her back cold comfort. Silent tears streamed down her cheeks so fast, it appeared as if their salty sadness could fill one of the waiting buckets.

Not wanting to rob Meggy of her few moments of private grief, Roddy remained where he was. The message, a worn piece of folded paper, seared his hand with the quick heat of jealousy. He guessed that the few words from afar penned there would make Meggy's heart soar higher than any words he might say to her face to face. But Roddy forced down

selfish thoughts of withholding the message. He could not deprive her of a bit of happiness in a time of such sorrow for her family. He began whistling softly, so she would have time to gather herself.

"Ah, there you are, Meggy. I thought I'd have to be searchin' every corner of Kerry for ye," he teased, not yet knowing how to show his feelings any other way.

Keeping her back to him, she mopped up her tears with her apron. Roddy continued his blarney. "Meggy, I would have climbed to the top of the Purple Mountains and swum the cold black of the lake to be deliverin' this message to ye."

It would have taken a girl with a much less curiosity than Meggy to ignore his mysterious words. Covering her sadness with crossness, she asked, "What is this message you're blatherin' on about?"

"Well, I'm fair sure it was not meant for a thorny-tongued girl. The Master would not be wastin' his words or his paper writin' to one as prickly as you," retorted Roddy.

The mere mention of the word "Master" had Meggy jumping to her feet. But when she reached to grab the message, Roddy held it high above her head. Even her dancing feet could not help her leap high enough to snatch it from his hand.

Then Roddy moved the message behind his back with one hand. With the other pressed to her forehead, he held Meggy at arm's length. "Relax," he advised, "don't be fussin' yourself. Would you care to be bargainin' with me for this message?"

Meggy stood, swinging at him, with arms that would never reach their target. "Why should I have to be bargainin' for somethin' that is meant for me?"

"Well now, that's a fine question, Meggy. The answer is simple. I've got it and you want it," smiled Roddy smugly.

This remark sent Meggy into another flurry of furious swings, cheeks flaming and green eyes snapping. "To think I'd begun believin' you might actually have the makin's of a fine young Irishman. Give me the message, you big, stupid amadon!"

"Meggy, Meggy didn't your mam ever tell ye that more is to be won by a sweet word or two than any of the nasty ones you can be stringin' together?" he scolded.

"Quit your yammerin', Roddy," she interrupted. "Spit it out. What do you want for givin' me me own message?"

"Just that you let me hold your hand while I walk ye home," requested Roddy.

She flew at him again in a fury of arms and legs. "What makes you think I'd hold your hand? The claw of a viviparous lizard would be far superior!"

"'Tis a simple bargain, Meggy. The message is yours for simply holdin' me hand."

Roddy's calmness infuriated her. "I must have the Master's message. Holdin' Roddy's hand just once couldn't be that bad," she thought. Aloud she said, "If that's the deal I'll be settin' some conditions of me own. First: you'll be takin' your hand off me head. I'll not be bargainin' under force. Second: I'll be holdin' your hand only this one time. Third: no one must see us holdin' hands. The minute anyone comes into view you will let go."

Putting out his hand Roddy said, "We'll make it official by shakin on it."

"No, we won't!" said Meggy, snatching the message away from him.

Sitting down, she carefully unfolded the worn-thin paper. Different scripts were crammed together. It appeared the first writer was a landlord demanding more soldiers. Meggy thought, "I hope his message was never delivered. Perhaps it wasn't, because here, right between his lines are the sweet words of an Irish lass writin' to her Frankie." Meggy had to look closely for Master Cleary's fine penmanship, and then she turned the paper round and round to follow the message, written around the edges.

Dear Meggy:

I hope this note finds you, your family and the McSorleys in good health.

"If you only knew," thought Meggy, wiping new-sprung tears.

As for myself, my wound improves daily. Without your quick actions the night I was shot, I would likely be without my arm now and perhaps even my life.

The letter shook as Meggy's hands trembled with fear.

◆

Last night, my host the shepherd returned with bad news. He had spotted our enemy near my hideaway. I must be disappearin' from here. Not for one more day can I allow this last link to lead our enemies from me to the shepherd and your families.

Until fate brings us back together,

Master Timothy Cleary

Meggy sat staring at the message. Her silent tears turned first to gulps and then to sobs that racked her body. "No, no, Master Cleary! Don't be leavin' me now—not with Da so sick. They all need me and I need you! I thought you'd be comin' back to us! I thought I could keep goin' until then! Now what am I goin' to do? Who will help me? I'm so tired. I'm worn out from the troubles and the tryin'. If only you could come just long enough to tell me what to do—how to go on without Da's help—without yours."

With no more words left to describe her fears and sorrows Meggy sobbed as if her heart were breaking. Roddy stood by helplessly. He wanted to comfort her. "But she made such a fuss about holdin' me hand that I'm afraid I'd only be makin' things worse," he thought.

He squatted beside her. Looking up at him, she threw her arms around his neck in a renewed bout of sobbing. Surprised, he continued to squat there silently, patting her back and stroking her curls until his legs were completely cramped.

◆

Gradually her sobs slowed down. He gave her his hankie. She blew and she wiped Suddenly realizing her position, Meggy backed up and looked into Roddy's face.

Although her eyes were ringed red, Roddy saw nothing but her beauty through her sadness. "Are ye feeling a bit better, Meggy? Is it bad news?"

She passed him the letter. "See for yourself, Roddy. He'll not be back."

After reading it, he said, "Meggy, it's not so bad. At least the Master is healin' well. He says he's only gone for now, that you'll be meetin' again."

She searched his eyes for a bit of hope. "Do you really think so? Why didn't he at least leave some wise words, tellin' me how we are to be gettin' along without him?"

"It's not like the Master to leave without a bit of advice. Let's look again, this time more carefully," suggested Roddy.

Right away she pointed to the bottom left-hand corner, "Is there somethin' there?"

"There are words across the corner, smudged perhaps by a thumb," replied Roddy.

"I think that's me name. It says, 'Meggy, remember, when times are darkest, turn to what you love best.'" She looked up at Roddy, "What do ye think he means?"

He answered, "I believe you will understand in time." Then taking her hand he headed them off towards home. Meggy left her hand in his all the way there, not once reminding him of the conditions of their agreement.

"Do ye mind, stoppin' in at Fiona's later and tellin' her I need her?" Meggy asked.

That was easy. Fiona was already hurrying along the path to the MacGillycuddys'. Roddy wondered if the girls would talk about him. He would have been disappointed. Meggy sat right down on the bench and read the Master's message to her best friend.

"'In times of trouble turn to what you love best.' Whatever do ye think he means?" Meggy asked.

"Why, it's your dancin'," answered Fiona. "You love nothin' more than that."

Rarely did the two best friends disagree, but Fiona's answer aggravated Meggy. "Fiona, it is as plain as the nose on your face that losing our home is the trouble. So Jesus, Mary and Joseph, how can me love of dancin' help with that?"

Fiona withdrew a paper from her pocket. "Perhaps you'll find your answer here."

With a disgusted sigh to show that she didn't believe any piece of paper could make bit of difference, Meggy took it and read.

With the mysterious passing of Dance Master Fancy Feet O'Flaherty, the sounds of dancing feet have been silenced in Kerry.

We know you'll be agreeing that Ireland is not its fine self without the dancing.

*Our young ones must not be allowed to grow up with-
out learning the jig and the reel.*

Therefore a new dance master must be found.
*As is our custom, a competition will be held at a date
and time that will find its way to you from Irish lips to
Irish ears.*

*The competitor who has the most dance steps in his
repertoire will win the right to teach our children and
earn a responsible rate of pay.*

*You'll not be needing the ghost of Fancy Feet to be
reminding you what could happen to anyone passing this
message or daring to teach our dances to Kerry's children.*

"That's all well and good for the man who wins the competition, but how is it goin' to keep a roof over the heads of
me and mine?" grumbled Meggy, crushing the paper.

Fiona was shocked. Meggy was always the first to solve a
problem, always the first to do what no one had ever done
before. That she could not see the possibility in the notice
made Fiona realize just how worn out with worry her best
friend was. So she spoke plainly. "I think you should enter
the competition. I believe you can win."

Meggy listened to Fiona. But her attitude did not change.
"Get your head out of the clouds, Fiona. There has never
been a female dance master and there never will be!"

Fiona replied quickly, with a barrage of questions, "Who
was County Kerry's first and finest dancin' lookout? Who

saved Master Cleary's life? Who took over as school teacher when our master had to escape? Was it a man who did all that?"

Meggy knew it wasn't a man. "I can hardly believe I did it. I feel so bone-tired, so sad. I can't imagine ever bein' that bold and brave again."

Fiona continued, "Now that Fancy Feet is gone, have you seen a man in all of Kerry who can dance better than ye?"

Meggy's pride as a dancer would only let her answer that question one way. "No."

"And do you think any man, no matter how fine a dancer, could teach our little ones to love the dancin' the way you do?"

"The children did seem to enjoy their dancin' lessons in our Crystal Cave school," replied Meggy modestly. She almost smiled, remembering her little students joyfully jigging and jumping on their rocky dance floor.

"Who do you think old Fancy Feet would want to take over his teachin' more than you, his finest student?" asked Fiona.

With her anger gone, Meggy reached out for her best friend's hand. "Thank ye for helpin' me see meself so bold and alive again. But now *I* have a question, Fiona: How will I ever get a chance to even enter a competition that has always been just for men?"

"I have the beginnin' of a plan, so don't be worryin' a hair on your head," explained Fiona, tugging a long dark curl.

With a hint of hope in her voice Meggy asked, "I've heard that even in these poor times, dance masters are still the highest paid of the travelers. Do ye think it might be enough to cover our rent—enough to keep me family from becomin' homeless?"

Fiona answered seriously, "I think it is the only way to earn it."

Both girls were silenced by the overwhelming need for Meggy to win this job. Fiona took a deep breath and went on. "For now, no one else in our village knows about the competition. I am this week's messenger. It is my responsibility to see that the news is read only by Irish eyes. So just say, 'Yes' and no one else will ever see this notice. Say, 'No', and I'll take it to the next drop-off. Then someone else who's yearnin' to become Kerry's dance master will have the chance."

The girls sat silently, the competition notice lying like a living being between them.

"Meggy, Meggy," called Mam from inside. With a quick hug, the girls left one another, but their thoughts stayed in the same place.

After getting Da settled in his chair, Meggy began asking her mother questions. "Have you ever been to a competition for a dance master?"

"Oh, yes, more than a few over me years. At times it seemed like one dance master was challengin' another every few weeks. The competitions always meant dancin' fun for all of us, but serious business for the masters. The loser had to move on, hopin' to win another area to teach in. But no one could defeat Fancy Feet. He was our dance master from before you were born."

"Is it true that dance masters are the best-paid travelers?" continued Meggy.

"You know how important it is to we Irish to keep our dances alive. As long as the people have coin to pay, they'll be payin' their dance masters. Why all these questions?" asked Mam, raising her eyebrows in her daughter's direction. Meggy needed to ask a most important question before she answered her mother's. "Has a female ever won a competition to become a dance master?"

Since Fancy Feet O'Flaherty had been waked on the very table they were sitting at, Vera MacGillycuddy began to suspect the direction of her once ever-dancing daughter's questions. "Well, me darlin', since I've not seen even one woman enter a competition, it follows that I've never seen a woman win."

"There are lots of wonderful female dancers," said Meggy. "Why don't they become dance masters, I mean dance mistresses?" asked Meggy.

"Well, aside from all the nonsense about things that men do and things that women do, the job of dance master can be a dangerous one—especially now,"cautioned Mam.

Glancing at her poor da, using up every ounce of his concentration in trying to put on his own boot, Meggy retorted, "It seems to me that many jobs are dangerous!"

And looking at her husband, oblivious to his family, Vera could not disagree. "To escape capture the dance masters travel alone, in the dark of night, from village to village. Unless a brave family allows them to sleep under their roof or in their barn, the masters usually sleep out under Kerry's skies, come stars or storms."

"Spendin' your days teachin' others how to dance can't be all bad. Never once did I see Dance Master O'Flaherty without a smile on his face," said Meggy.

Mam, too, got caught up in the memories, "When he came to tea, he only talked of students, especially you me darlin', his finest pupil."

"Wouldn't it be lovely to spend your days doin' what you love most?" sighed Meggy.

When her husband stirred, Vera moved closer to her daughter. "So, Meggy," she said in a no-nonsense voice, "where are they holdin' the competition to replace Fancy Feet?"

Meggy blushed, "I don't know yet, Mam. Fiona picked up the notice today. It said the time and place will be passed later from Irish lips to Irish ears."

"Speakin' of ears, you'd best not let your father hear of this. No point in upsettin' him now, as it is highly unlikely you will even be allowed to compete," warned Mam.

With her fingers crossed and her toes crossed, Meggy asked, "Does this mean I have your permission to enter and then become a dance master?"

"One thing at a time," answered her mother. "First the competition and then…we'll see. But no matter what, I want you to know how proud I am of you, for tryin'."

Honest as always, Meggy admitted, "If not for Fiona I probably wouldn't have."

"Sometimes our friends know more about what we can do than we know ourselves. Now off you go to tell Fiona. You've already got stars in your eyes, so you'll be no good to me this afternoon anyway," said Mam, giving her daughter a quick hug.

Dancing out the door she ran into a red-haired whirlwind. Then like a will-o-the-wisp she was gone. Her brother asked, "Mam, where is Meggy goin'? Why didn't she take me?"

His mother distracted him, "Perhaps it was because there's enough dirt under your nails to plant taties and your shoes smell like cow plops."

Dan had scrubbed both sets of fingernails before he realized his mother had not answered his question. Wiping his hands on his trousers he raced off down the path. He had his own idea about where he might find Meggy.

In the meantime his sister was halfway to Fiona's. With her black curls flying and steps so light they barely touched the leaves, she could have been mistaken for a wood nymph, by those who still believed.

Having sensed Meggy coming, in the way only best friends can, Fiona was waiting. One look at her friend's face and she knew there would be a female competitor in the dance master competition. Taking Meggy's outstretched hand as she flew by, the two were off to their special place under the Crystal Cave Crankanny tree.

Once there, Fiona made the unusual move of speaking first, "I've all the jobs figured out. You'll need someone to play your dance music and somethin' special to wear. All dance masters wear something fanciful. Remember the bells that always jingled on Fancy Feet's toes and round his belly?"

"Fiona! Where do you think I'll be findin' an accompanist and a costume? The only thing special about my dresses is that one is holey and the other is holier," snorted Meggy.

Rolling her eyes at her friend's bad joke, Fiona went on, "You need not worry. Just concentrate on your dancin'. I'll be takin' care of the rest—including somethin' fanciful."

"But Fiona, how can I be practicin' without an accompanist?" questioned Meggy.

"Well, the handiest and most obvious choice is…," began Fiona.

"Tell me you're not suggestin' Dan," interrupted Meggy. "He can't keep a secret any longer than it takes him to run to the privy and back!"

"Give your brother a chance. He kept our 'Red Witch Catchin' Plan' a secret. And he did a fine job playin' for your Crystal Cave dance classes, didn't he now?" asked Fiona.

"He did quickly master the simple tunes for the little ones," agreed Meggy. "But to win this contest I will have to go far beyond simple. Do you think he could keep up?"

"I could! I could!" said Dan, half-falling on the girls from his eavesdropping post on a branch above them. He had beat them to their secret spot by taking the shortcut.

Taking a good look at her brother, Meggy knew it was time to trust him. "Alright Dan, you will be my accompanist."

With one quick flip, her accompanist disappeared as quickly as a leprechaun.

"Our plan is coming together," said Fiona, "Can you and Dan begin tomorrow?"

Meggy's mind was so full she didn't even answer Fiona. Turning toward home, her mind was humming. Her heart was singing.

Meggy was preparing to dance again. Dance as she'd never danced before.

4

❖

The Dream

Even though the bench she slept on was hard, Meggy spent the night dancing in her dreams. Perhaps because her only music was the hens cooing gently below, her dream dances were not fast and furious. The steps she took were soft, like tiptoeing on clouds and her leaps like soaring with the wind. Her arms moved, not like a whirling dervish, but more like feathers, floating, gently sheltering the dancer and those lucky enough to watch.

Fiona, on the other hand, had not slept at all. Her mind was whirling. With the same strong belief she had that Meggy could win the competition, she believed she could handle her responsibilities. Promising her best friend she would take care of the costume was as easy as predicting

Kerry's rain. Finding a way to convince County Kerry's folk to allow a female to compete, however, would take some talking as fancy as Fancy Feet's footwork. Keeping soldiers and informers away from the competition would require both brains and bodies.

Only Meggy's mam and Dan were up when Fiona arrived the next morning.

"Come in, darlin'. Any day that begins with your sweet face at our door is bound to be a good one," Mrs. MacGillycuddy said.

Meggy did not want to wake up. She wanted to continue dancing on clouds. But ten cold tickling fingers rudely dragged her from her dream's heavenly warmth.

Catching a wink from her best friend, Meggy stopped her squawking and threats to throw her little brother into the lake and got to work. They got Da up and washed while Mam prepared breakfast. Meggy ate her mush quickly while helping her father. With Dan sorting bogwood and Da napping Meggy told her mother and friend about her dream.

"My steps were so soft, like dancin' on down. When I spun, my toes whirled so fast, me head popped through a low cloud. Me arms felt longer and lighter than ever before. I know I'm to share this heavenly dance," said Meggy.

Looking at her friend's glowing face, Fiona said, "Your dream was a message. Now I know what your costume should be like. Your mam and me will be takin' care of it."

Meggy was puzzled. "Fiona, how can you know what to

make, when I know only bits and pieces of me dream dance?"

When silence was all she got from her best friend, Meggy turned to her mam, and intercepted a secret nod between them.

"Darlin' girl," said her mother, "you're doin' all this work to win the competition for us. Don't deny us the pleasure of makin' just the costume you need. You trust us to do that for you, don't ye ?"

"Oh, Mam, of course I trust you and Fiona. I know every stitch will be lovely. But you already work from dawn to dusk, caring for Da. How will ye find time to be makin' me a costume?" Meggy was worried about her mam, who grew more bent-over each day.

"For as long as it takes, I'll be here to help. Your mam and I will take turns sewin' and doin' for your da," added Fiona.

"Well, I guess there is nothin' left for me to do, except prepare me dances. I don't know if I can face day after day of dancin', dancin' and dancin' some more," she said. With a wide wink and a toss of her black curls as she skipped outdoors.

Quickly closing both halves of the door, Fiona whispered to Mrs. MacGillycuddy, "I think Meggy's dream means she is meant to dance as an angel."

"Aren't you clever? She did say clouds and use the word heavenly. And don't I have just the perfect material," said Mam, with more lilt in her voice than had been there since the accident. Bending over the chest at the end of the bed, she lifted something up onto her arms and then presented it to Fiona.

The girl gasped. It was the MacGillycuddys' one treasure, their one link to the past and better times—their handmade white lace tablecloth. "Oh, no—not that—we can't be cuttin' up your family's fine lace!"she exclaimed.

"We can and we will, Fiona." Mrs. MacGillycuddy spoke firmly of the cloth that was all she had left of her own mother. "What good will a lace tablecloth be to a family that has no home, let alone a table! If Meggy is allowed to compete…if she wins…"

Fiona held up one end of the finely stitched lace. Studying it, she said, "The shoulder line could be here if we fold it this way."

Mam joined in, "Yes, that's it. Then we could cut it all of one piece, and make it like a tunic to wear over her dress. The only sewin' would be on the sides and the long, full sleeves."

Fiona fingered it thoughtfully, "If we cut carefully and bind the loose edges, we might be able to sew it back together again—later."

Cupping Fiona's face in her rough hands, Vera said, "There are two angels involved with this costume—one who dances like an angel and the other who thinks like one."

Lowering her eyes and blushing, Fiona moved toward the door. "There are more things I need to help Meggy win. So if you don't need me, I'll be off."

Fiona flitted from one cottage to another. At each she

asked for the same thing but gave no reason for the asking. Some gave right away and others said to come back later. The few she got about half-filled her pocket. Fall's damp air poked its icy fingers through the holes in her dress and made her bone-thin back ache with the cold. She used to have a little meat on her bones from often sharing the MacGillycuddys' meals. But now they had barely enough for themselves.

Approaching the pub she spotted the McSorleys, father and son, loading up their donkey. "Perhaps the chill will make me cheeks rosy," thought Fiona. Even though she knew Meggy did not want Roddy, she kept her crush to herself.

It was his father who called out, with a chuckle in his voice, "And what brings such a pretty lass into the company of two rogues and their ass?"

Shyness overcame Fiona and she stood speechless on the spot.

"Don't tell me we've been blessed with the company of that most rare creature, a female who doesn't chatter like a magpie?" asked Mr. McSorley of his son.

"'Tis just Fiona, Da. She's not used to talkin', bein' always with Meggy, the Queen of the Magpies," answered Roddy.

His "just Fiona" made her heart and her hopes sink a little. She motioned the men to join her behind the donkey. In whispers, she explained Meggy's plans to compete in the dance competition. Unfortunately, they did not notice Seamus Fox, just inside the pub's back door, straining his big

informer's ears to hear what he hoped were secret plans.

Considering Fiona's plan Mr. McSorley said, "I might question the wisdom of Meggy becomin' a travelin' dance master if she had not so bravely outwitted that brute of a soldier, on the Night of the Banshee." Nodding, he continued, "The long night journeys and constant hidin' are not for the faint of heart. But I can think of no one braver." Putting his hands on Fiona's thin shoulders, he asked, "What can we do to help?"

"I need the two of you for a most important task," Fiona answered, and then lowered her voice to tell them what she planned. "If it doesn't work, I'll need someone to tell them how Meggy trapped the traitorous Red Witch."

"I'd be proud to tell that tale," said Roddy.

"Then all will know she is brave and clever. But how will they know what an amazin' dancer she is?" asked Fiona.

"Well, I could tell how Fancy Feet himself was always braggin' that Meggy was not only the finest dancer in the village, but in all of County Kerry too. That is a fittin' recommendation," said Mr. McSorley with satisfaction.

Fiona's next request required not only brains but bodies. "Could the two of you and a few trustworthy men keep any but our people from getting to the competition?"

"With pleasure," answered Roddy. He was already plotting a herd of stubborn cows blocking one road and perhaps a tipped cart of rutabagas, the other. Drawing closer to Roddy, Fiona asked for a second, much smaller favor.

He agreed happily, "While makin' me deliveries I'll gather a rainbow of those for Meggy."

Fiona beamed as she walked away, her plan was coming together so well. She was unaware of Seamus following her as she skipped back to the MacGillycuddys' cottage. Dan rushed past her at full speed. Worried that Meggy's father had taken another turn for the worse, she hurried too.

With Mr. MacGillycuddy snoring in his chair, Dan was teasing Meggy and Mam. "Guess what I heard passin' from Irish lips to Irish ears at the pub?" He waited to be coaxed into telling more.

"Tell us Dan, just tell us," urged his none-too-patient sister.

Meggy was backed up by a simple "Now!" from their mam.

Dan delivered his news with a flourish, "Ladies, thanks to me you will be one of the first to know that the dance competition will be held at the crossroads—Sunday next."

"Sunday next!" exclaimed the three females. "How will we finish the costume by then?" groaned Mam.

"How will I learn me dances by then?" gasped Meggy.

"Will the secret part of me plan arrive by then?" sighed Fiona, so softly that no one asked her what she meant.

"All we can do is begin," said Meggy, running out the door and down the path to her favorite dancing spot. Dan was right behind her.

They were going too fast to notice the sneaky Fox, ducking around the corner of their cottage. Though he had pressed his dirty ear to the window wall he had heard not a word. In a frustrated fury, Seamus turned to leave and slipped on Dan's collection of wet acorns and mudpies. When he landed his back, cramped and like a tipped turtle, he could not get up.

That is how Roddy found him. Totally embarrassed Seamus snarled, "Tell one person about this and I'll make sure Lord Black knows of your father's secret business."

Knowing Fox could not go one day without his delivery of their poteen (the finest liquor made in Kerry) Roddy ignored the threat. Flipping Seamus over with his foot, he waited till the traitor crawled out of sight before knocking on the MacGillycuddys' door.

Speaking low in case any big-eared traitors dared return, Roddy said, "Fiona, we've set the seeds of your plan in place—the others are happy to help. Anyone who wants to pass through the crossroads Sunday next will find their trip somewhat disturbed."

When Roddy winked at her to seal their secret partnership, Fiona was so flustered all she could do was nod. By the time she was able to speak, his attention was back to where it always was. "Mrs. MacGillycuddy, could you be tellin' me where Meggy is?"

He and Meggy's mam were both taken aback when Fiona answered, "She's practicin' her dancin', Roddy and I'd thank ye kindly not to be disturbin' her."

And practicing she was. Meggy and Dan had returned to

the Crystal Cave where they had had their hiding school. In that secret and safe haven, the two could dance and play their hearts out. Dan's early wrong notes and Meggy's small missteps would be kept forever secret by the bats who swooped overhead like supervising dance masters.

Dan played better with each practice, coaxing his notes to their sweetest trills. His sister's feet flew faster and faster in their intricate steps. As a female competitor, Meggy knew she needed to have not only the most steps but also the most original and the best.

With every leap, his sister soared so high and so far that Dan was afraid she might bump her head on a stalactite, or fly right off the end of their tablerock dance floor.

"Meggy, be careful," he warned. "It's some ugly-lookin' dancer you'll be with bumps on your head and bruises on your knees."

Everyday they practiced till Meggy's feet were covered with blisters and Dan's fingertips were swollen. They stopped only to redo a bar of music or a step that didn't work. Brother and sister, they were each other's coaches, audience and biggest fans.

Finally the last day came. They did not drag themselves out of the cave until dusk.

Tomorrow they would have a new audience. Tomorrow Dan would play, while Meggy danced the dance of her life.

5

❖

The Traitor

The MacGillycuddys' cottage hummed with energy and excitement. Before breakfast was even ready, Dan was dancing a jig and playing his whistle at the same time. Fiona was already there to help. Although Meggy's da usually slept most of the day, that morning he awoke with a roar that stopped all where they stood. When Vera saw her husband put his hands over his ears and rock back and forth in pain, she knew his terrible headaches had returned.

She tried gently massaging his temples, but he shoved her away. Dan, who had never seen his father treat his mother like that, dropped his whistle into the big pot. The echoing clatter sent his father into a complete rage. Mac grabbed the pen and on several scraps of paper wrote angry, hurtful words: *Can't sleep—bad noisy son—chattering daughter—wife lets strangers in—GET OUT—GET OUT—GET OUT OF MY HOUSE!*

Mam gently guided a white-faced Dan out the back door and then returned to calm his father. Meggy, who had been standing on a stool while Fiona pinned her costume, fell in her hurry to get out and away from the raging man. She got up with a sore knee, dirt on her lace costume and a terrible ache in her heart.

Fiona's own cottage was often filled with the roaring of an angry man. She asked, "Is your leg all right? Will you be up to the dancin' tonight?"

At her friend's soft words Meggy began to cry, "Just look! Me knee is bleedin'. I've dirtied the white lace tunic you worked so hard on." But not even to Fiona could she admit how much her father's anger beat the dancing right out of her.

Clucking around Meggy like a mother hen, Fiona wiped the dirt off the tunic and the tears from her face. By the time she finished cleansing her friend's knee, Da's anger was spent. Knowing there was nothing they could do about what had just happened, Fiona decided it would be best to go ahead with their plans. "Meggy, I've got a surprise for ye."

"I've had quite enough surprises for today, thank ye," said Meggy sharply.

Ignoring her friend's attitude Fiona went on, "Did you ever think, it bein' all white, that your tunic might be needin' a bit of color?"

Meggy answered, "Havin' a costume at all was more than I ever hoped for."

"Then it's a good thing I hoped for more for ye!" said Fiona saucily. "Close your eyes and hold out your hands." She pulled a ball of many colors out of her pocket. Having often imagined this moment, she could not wait one minute more. "Open your eyes!"

Looking down, Meggy saw what appeared to be a round rainbow. The look on her face changed from discouragement to delight.

Fiona reached in and tugged free a scarlet end. Taking the ball back into her own hands, she gave Meggy the loose end and said, "Dance!"

As she skipped and leapt, the ball of ribbon unraveled and shone in the light. Forest green followed scarlet. Sunshine yellow followed purple. Each scrap of ribbon was tied with a tiny knot to the next. Wrapping the ribbons round and round herself, Meggy stopped and asked breathlessly, "Where did you get them? What are they for?"

"Each treasured bit of color came from a family that wants to help you and yours. They all gave trustingly because I dared not tell what they were givin' for," said Fiona, proud of the kindness of their neighbors.

"Well, do ye think it might be time to be tellin' me what they are for?" asked Meggy, whose spirits were now as bright as the ribbons.

"Keep those dancin' feet still for a minute, and I'll show

ye," answered Fiona, enjoying every moment of her surprise. As swift as the swallows in the spring, her fingers wove the ribbons back and forth, weaving the two front pieces of the lace tunic together.

Reaching out to hug her best friend, Meggy said, "Oh Fiona, I never imagined my costume could be so beautiful. You've got magic in your fingers."

"Now you just be stayin' still a bit longer, I'm not done yet," said the young seamstress as she wove ribbons in and out around the wide bottom of each lace sleeve. Then she tied them off, leaving long ends of different lengths and colors hanging down.

The minute Fiona's fingers stopped tying, Meggy's feet started twirling. She spread her arms wide spinning and twirling like a whirlwind of ribbon and raven black curls. "Let's go show Dan," she said. "I think he's out back." The two of them tiptoed round the cottage to surprise and cheer up her little brother.

They could see neither hide nor hair of him. But when they were quiet they could hear strange, sad sounds from the privy. They were notes from a whistle, combined with the sobs and snuffles of a sad young boy.

"Dan, come out and see our surprise," coaxed Fiona. Grateful that someone had finally come to find him, Dan didn't need much coaxing. He stopped suddenly in the privy doorway, dazzled by a whirl of white wings and bright ribbons. "Meggy, you look like an angel," he gasped.

"She does indeed,"sighed their mother who had just stepped out back to see how her children were doing.

Meggy turned toward her in gratitude, "Oh, Mam. How can I ever thank you for givin' up your lace tablecloth, your one treasure?"

"Just seeing you dancin' with such joy again is thanks enough,"said her mother.

As if by silent vow, no one spoke of their father's rage—not that day, not ever.

"Meggy, take off your tunic. I'll hide it under the eggs in me basket," said Mam.

Reaching out for the basket Danny announced, "I'll carry the basket tonight."

"Oh no, you won't," gasped his mother and sister, with visions of egg yolk on white lace. Spotting the grin on his face, they knew Dan was teasing and joined him, laughing.

After the grim start to their day, the mother was glad to hear her children laughing. She allowed herself a moment to wonder if their father would ever laugh with them again, before turning her daughter toward the door. "Come in, so I can tame those wild curls of yours. It is a long walk to the crossroads and you'll need to eat somethin' before we go."

Fiona said, "I've a job to do, so I'll be off for now." Thrilled with the success of her plans so far, she practically flew along the path to the well. She knew the women gathered there at this time of the day, to catch up on the news as well as fill their buckets.

What she didn't know was that Seamus Fox spotted her leaving the MacGillycuddys' cottage. He knew something was up when he saw her run bucketless toward the well. The moment Fiona joined them, the women flocked round her till she disappeared in a circle of skirts and shawls. Seamus, hiding behind a wagon, heard only soft clucking and cackling. "The old biddies," he scowled. But as a pair of women headed home, past his hiding place, he heard one word—crossroads.

"Crossroads? Why would they be talking about the cross-roads?" Seamus wondered. He might not have figured any-thing out at all, if a gust of fall wind had not carried one cheery voice right to his traitorous ears, "Wish Meggy good luck."

"Aha! Now I just might know why their darling Meggy needs luck at the crossroads. If what I think is true, I'll need reinforcements before I head there too. I wonder if Miss Meggy will like having the lord's soldiers as her dancing partners?" gloated Seamus wickedly and aloud.

Now Roddy, who had hurried to catch up with Fiona and had seen Seamus eavesdropping in his hiding place, saw by the sly look on the treacherous Fox's face that he had likely guessed their plan.

"I think not," he growled, answering Seamus's question.

So sure of himself and so stupid was Seamus Fox that he taunted Roddy, "Well, McSorley, no doubt you're in on tonight's secret. Perhaps you will pass my message on to your beloved Meggy. Just tell her to save the last dance for me."

Roddy knew he must stop Seamus from getting to the

manor and collecting Lord Black's gang of thugs. The thought of their sleazy hands on Meggy made his blood boil. The lazy Seamus, who made his living with his secrets and lies, was no match for the hardworking young McSorley. One trip and a push was all it took for Roddy to put Fox's smug face in the dirt.

While Fox was too stunned to fight back, Roddy yanked him up with his back to the well. He held him there with one hand while he pulled the bucket up. Using Seamus's neckcloth, Roddy tied his hands around the bucket rope. In one quick movement he lifted the poor excuse of a man onto the bucket, a leg on either side of the rope. Removing the foppish sash Fox wore around his waist, Roddy used it to bind his ankles together.

Seamus begged, "Please, McSorley, I beg of you—please don't leave me to drown."

"You were going to leave Meggy with Lord Black's evil soldiers to be thrown into the dungeon or worse," said Roddy. "You deserve to drown like the rat you are." Roddy planned just to scare Fox and keep him away from the competition. But he decided to keep that bit of information from his sniveling prisoner.

Seamus's calls for help were muffled by his hankie stuffed into his mouth.

"What a pleasure to shut your betrayin', tale-tellin' gob," said Roddy. Using every bit of strength in his strong young back and arms, he slowly lowered Fox into the well. When he heard the water smacking against the bottom of the bucket he stopped and secured the rope around a sturdy oak tree. Looking down he could see Seamus's legs jerking and splashing in the water. "Use your head, man!" he advised. "The less you move the less strain you put on the rope. You wouldn't want it to be givin' way now, would you? Now I'll be off to warn the villagers not to be usin' this well. I'll tell them a sick balck rat must have fallen in, as it seems to have developed a terrible stink."

"We'll see if he's a changed man when I bring some lads to haul him up," Roddy told himself. Then he headed off to help with the roadblocks. Needing to keep Meggy and their secret visitor safe, they could take no chance of any soldiers or informers getting through.

Knowing his father and a crew of men were making the north and east roads passable only to their own kind, Roddy went southwest. Heading up the south road he soon heard the baaing of sheep, a lot of sheep. Rounding a curve, he could not help but laugh. A bottleneck of black-faced sheep were caught in the narrow gap between two steep hillsides. Recognizing Roddy, the lookout cawed like a crow and two shepherds appeared.

"Ah, it's just young McSorley. We were hopin' for a soldier or two, perhaps even Lord Black himself," chuckled one ruddy faced shepherd.

"I brought me ram, Teddy, along," added another. "He's been having uncontrollable urges to connect his horns to the seat of a Redcoat's pants ever since two tried to ride him."

"Me dogs will make those black-faced woollies mind. Here's a family of our own, all decked out for some dancin'," said the shepherd. He whistled and from behind an outcropping of rock, two dogs appeared and stood, ears pricked, waiting for his command.

The shepherd's words were too low for Roddy to hear but the next thing he knew, the dogs had created a passage from one end of the gap to the other. The minute the family passed through a second command was whistled and the opening disappeared as if it had never been there. Roddy wished he could stay and watch the Redcoats try to deal with this troop of curly-horned mountain sheep and Teddy too.

Feeling sure no enemies would get through this crossroads, Roddy cut through the woods to check on the road from the west. This time no sounds met him, but as he got close, a terrible smell assaulted his nose. Stepping out of the woods he saw a wagon that had tipped its load of dung all across the narrow road. There was not a soul in sight. The scene looked as if the driver had gone off on his donkey for help.

But when Roddy whistled Copperkin's secret signal, a man popped up behind the thorn-thick hedges on each side of the road. One chuckled, "Wouldn't ye just love to see Seamus tryin' to tiptoe through that load. He'll not be gettin' past us, will he now?"

"Sure and he won't," laughed Roddy, knowing that Seamus wouldn't even get close.

"But how will our own get through?"

Like a leprechaun, the other man disappeared from behind the thorny hedge and popped up in front of it. "What do you think of our secret, 'Irish Only' door, Roddy? We've another carved out, just beyond our sweet smellin' tip-up."

"I think your cleverness is bettered only by your smell," laughed Roddy as he turned and began running back toward the village. "I must hurry to the MacGillycuddys' so I can take our competitor to the crossroads," planned Roddy, who trusted no one but himself to keep his Meggy safe.

At that very moment on the north road, his father was interrogating a stranger, who had introduced himself grandly as John James O'Sullivan, Ireland's Finest Dance Master. Never liking a braggart Roddy's da asked plainly, "Well if you're the Finest Dance Master in Ireland why do you need be competin' here, for our dance master position?"

The broad-chested man was also being challenged by a gaggle of hissing geese. They stood guard around him, pecking their reflections in his shiny shoes and tugging at his cloak.

Insulted, O'Sullivan threw one end of his cape across his other shoulder and replied in a huff, "If you have quite finished your inquisition, I must be on my way."

Mr. McSorley was taking great pleasure in not only delaying Meggy's competitor but also sending the man off to the crossroads much less confident than when he had arrived. It

seemed that a big gander shared Mr. McSorley's attitude. He had already attached himself to the stranger's ample buttocks and now chased him down the road.

After a quick stop to pick up the cart and donkey at the pub, Roddy made it to the MacGillycuddys' just as they were heading off. Taking off his cap, he bowed and said, "Miss Meggy, may I have the pleasure of deliverin' ye to the crossroads?"

"I'm not a load of dung or poteen that needs deliverin', Roddy McSorley! I'll be walkin' with me family," answered Meggy, who was too nervous to handle any change in plans.

Fiona spoke up, "Acceptin' a ride would be a smart idea, Meggy. It's a long walk and you need to be savin' your feet for the dancin'."

"I agree," said Meggy's mam. "And you will be stayin' much cleaner and prettier than if you walked all the way on the dusty road."

Before Meggy could say "but" Danny added, "You'll not want me arrivin' at the crossroads with me throat too filled with dust to be playin' for you, will ye?"

"I'll not be ridin' while Fiona, Mam and Dan walk. I would not be dancin' today if not for them. Since you've not room for all to ride, all of us will walk," said Meggy firmly.

"Meggy, you're as stubborn as a mule, but you're wrong. You, Fiona and your mam will ride in the cart. Dan will be happy to ride Bess. I'll lead and walk from the side." Before Meggy could think of another reason to disagree, Roddy swooped a laughing Dan up on Bessie's back. As he kindly assisted Fiona and Mam into the cart, Meggy knew she would be riding that day. She sat back snug and warm between them, closed her eyes and ran over the steps in her mind, until her spirits too were dancing.

6

❖

DUELING DANCERS

The closer they got to the crossroads the busier the road became. With baskets and stools, grannies and babies, families came from the north, south, east and west. Some had been walking the dusty roads since breakfast. Others joined in when friends passed their doors. Young ones, whose little feet could not walk another step, were perched on big brothers' shoulders or carried by sisters not much bigger than they. Although the sun was still bright, the frosty air of the coming night nipped small ears and bare toes. Neither distance nor cold could have kept these Kerry folk from the competition and the dancing that would follow.

When Roddy and his passengers arrived, the others got out to visit with friends from neighboring villages. Meggy chose to wait in the cart, huddled into her gran's black shawl, studying the faces of those gathering. She needed to see them all, know them as friend or foe. What she did not know was that one other wore a disguise, a disguise much like hers.

Meggy searched for the unwelcome face of Seamus Fox, thinking, "For the last week he's stuck to me like a burr on a sheep's tail. If he found out about the competition and has sent for Lord Black's soldiers to arrest me, I'll end the night as a prisoner instead of a dance mistress." She raged silently, "How can it be that we have to send secret messages, set up roadblocks, and post lookouts just to spend an evenin' dancin' our own dances, in our own way, in our own country? What kind of cruelness punishes a dance master with imprisonment or worse just for teachin' children the joy of the jig or the reel?"

When an unfamiliar man came into view, Meggy stopped her fretting to study him. With his cloak of many colors and highly polished shoes, he was definitely not a villager. The stranger approached woman after woman, with what must have been compliments, as he left most of them blushing or smiling.

"Could this man be a spy or a dance competitor? I need to get close enough to hear what he's sayin'." By pulling the shawl over her head and walking bent as an old hag, she slipped through the crowd unnoticed.

Then the stranger began introducing himself to the men. His soft hands and bright clothing set him apart from them, like a showhorse in a team of workhorses. But his tales of traveling adventures soon drew the men to him as his compliments had drawn the women.

Meggy studied him as one dancer would another. "He stands as if he owns the earth." She took a closer look. "Wouldn't I love havin' shoes so new I could see me face in their shine? But…is that swellin', where his shoes bind his feet? And the way his belly slips out, below his vest…the competitor is overly fond of his food."

Others were searching the crowd. Roddy was at the top of the tallest oak, its last leaves offering poor camouflage. He wanted to be down with Meggy. "But from up here," he told himself, "I can make sure no enemy gets close. I failed her once as lookout, but not today—not ever again."

On the ground, Fiona's eyes raced through the crowd, searching for the one person who could make a difference should Meggy not be allowed to compete. Stepping onto a stump she searched for a familiar head above the crowd. Back at ground level, she saw Mrs. McSorley leading a once-tall, but now much-bent-over woman. Ever kind, she went and took a firm hold of the old one's other arm.

The woman jerked her arm back and uttered a surprisingly deep cry of pain. All eyes turned toward them. Realizing suddenly who was under that black shawl, Fiona knew attention was the last thing they needed. Quietly, she led the women to the stump and seated them with their backs to the crowd. Kneeling, looking up into the "old one's" face, she whispered, "Master Cleary, please forgive me for hurtin' your arm. Thank you for so bravely riskin' your life to be here today."

Taking her cold hands into his, the master looked down into her dear loyal face and said, "Fiona, it is you who are truly bright and brave. Without your plans, none of this would be happening. Now just relax and let the rest of us do our parts."

Mr. McSorley announced, "Gather round—the competition is about to begin. As you know, we're needin' a dance master to replace the dear departed Fancy Feet O'Flaherty. The dancer who wins this competition will become Kerry's newest dance master. Now let the first competitor step forward and introduce himself."

As the stranger confidently made his way to the front, the crowd parted for him as the Red Sea had for Moses. The man's compliments and tales had paid off. The women clapped and the men patted his back. His name was on all tongues: "O'Sullivan, O'Sullivan, John James O'Sullivan."

With a dramatic swish of his cloak, he turned towards them. "Thank ye, fine people of Kerry. Never have I seen a county so blessed with beautiful women."

"Enough blarney, O'Sullivan. Tell us of your work," instructed Mr. McSorley.

O'Sullivan puffed out his red-vested chest till he looked like a banty rooster at mating time. "I've taught for ten years and in as many counties. As the finest of all artificial rhythmical walkers I leave each county with new steps, the likes of which they've never danced before."

Questions rustled through the crowd. "Why is it that he moves so often?" "Perhaps he pays too much attention to the women and not enough to the dancin'." "Fancy Feet O'Flaherty was with us for twenty years." "And in the end only Death beat him."

Fiona left Mrs. McSorley and the tall black-shawled crone. Making her way through the crowd, she stood behind a small black-shawled crone, whose right leg was jiggling.

"O'Sullivan, are you ready?" asked Mr. McSorley.

"I am supremely confident in my ability to challenge any competitor," answered O'Sullivan. He winked cockily, as if the thought of anyone challenging him in turn was a joke.

Then Roddy's da asked, "Are there any who will accept O'Sullivan's challenge?"

All were quiet. Careful not to disturb the rainbow of ribbons tied into Meggy's curls, Fiona lifted the shawl off her friend's head. All gasped at the transformation. Where once had stood a small black-shawled hag, was now a raven-haired beauty, dressed in white lace and ribbons.

As Meggy stepped with quiet grace to the front, a rumble of words raced through the crowd. "Why, it's a young woman!" "Aye, and a lovely one at that." Then, louder still: "Lovely or not, what does she think she's doin'?" "Only a man can compete." "Only a man can be dance master!"

Then came a few voices of recognition from the people of

Copperkin. "That's our Meggy!" "So that is what young Fiona needed the ribbons for!" "That rose ribbon is from me gran's wedding shawl."

Mr. McSorley tried to proceed with his questions. But before Meggy could even speak her name, she was shouted down by men chanting, "A man for master!" "We want a man for dance master!"

Just when she was considering retreating back into the crowd, Mr. McSorley broke through the shouting. "Stop your yammerin', ye fools. There is nothin' written that says a dance master must be a man. This competitor will be judged by her ability to meet the challenge or not. O'Sullivan, are you willin' to compete against Miss Meggy?"

Not only did O'Sullivan have talented feet, but he also had a crafty mind. Graciously he faced the crowd. "She's as brave as she is beautiful, isn't she? Of course, I'll accept her as my competitor."

O'Sullivan's apparent generosity earned him applause from the crowd. Meggy gave him a pretty curtsey, even though she hated him patting her head as if she was a stray dog that needed his charity. He was well-pleased with himself. "I could beat that skinny peasant girl if I had to dance on one foot. And now I have the crowd's favor too," he thought. And at the next words from the crowd, he added to himself, "I may not have to face any competition at all."

"Even if this girl meets the dance challenge, she could never travel from village to village through the perils of night," said a man from the next village. "Even O'Flaherty ended up dead in a ditch. How can she be brave enough to face dangers perhaps worse than death at the hands of enemy soldiers?"

When it seemed no one could imagine this, and the murmuring began to rise, Mr. McSorley motioned Roddy to come down. Danny and the tall old woman also stepped forward. At one nod from her, Mr. McSorley stopped Roddy and beckoned the crone forward. When she dropped her shawl and stood up straight, the crowd was shocked to silence again. In her place stood Master Cleary. All knew he had been shot. Many had feared he was dead. Everyone, especially Meggy, knew he was risking his life to be there. Her heart pounded with fear and joy. "You're here. You're here," was all she could think.

All listened respectfully when Maser Cleary spoke. "I suspect you've heard my tale, 'The Night of the Banshee.' It began under the Crankanny Tree, where the Stony Books are stacked. The heroine is a lovely lass with raven-black hair and laughin' green eyes. She loved three things: her wee brother, her larnin' and her dancin'. When enemies tried to destroy that which she held dear, she fought back with the power of her love, her mind and her dancin' feet.

"As County Kerry's first dancing lookout, she stomped out a warning that saved her fellow students and myself from imprisonment or worse. But did that brave girl choose to save herself, then? No. She stayed until the last little one had been hauled up over the clifftop to safety.

"That would have been enough to declare this brave-hearted miss a hero, but my story is far from told. With the children, including her own small brother, now running down the path to home, she was again free to save herself. But the boom of a gun turned her back—back to me, as I fell with my life's blood running from me.

"Not even when we heard the shouts and curses of the enemy coming closer and closer did this child desert me. Instead, she managed to drag me to the far side of the field. When the soldiers turned away from us, we thought we might be safe. But then one angry man with a gun reared his ugly head. My heroine led the brute away from me by transforming herself into a terrifying apparition that danced like the wind and howled like a banshee. The cowardly bully screamed in terror as he disappeared down into the dark and dangerous gloom of the cliff.

"I'll never forget the darlin' green-eyed banshee who saved me life and danced her way into me heart forever." With a flourish of his good arm Master Cleary announced, "That brave girl stands before you today! She is our own Miss Meggy!"

Meggy's heart soared as the crowd clapped and cheered. Her own bravery, as told by Master Cleary, had won her the right to compete.

Now totally ignored by his fair-weather friends, the flashy O'Sullivan's graciousness disappeared. He grumbled, "So what if Miss Meggy was brave? I've been travelin' since before she wore her first nappie. I've faced many a danger."

Mr. McSorley announced, "It's time to begin, Miss Meggy and Mister John James O'Sullivan." Two strong men approached, each carrying a half-door on his head. "Our dance floors are now in place. Gran Ryan, once County Kerry's finest dancer, will mark an X for each misstep. Each new step will be marked by a stroke in the road."

As O'Sullivan's fiddler sat tuning up, the crowd settled in. Little ones sat in laps, men stood and young women leaned back into their sweethearts' arms. The two competitors took their places. Mr. McSorley continued. "Begin with the seven basic steps." The minute one dancer completed their step the other followed, always trying to better their competitor's last. Both moved quickly and confidently through sidesteps and hops.

The protesters, now silent, watched the two pairs of dancing feet intently. There were five who watched with their hearts as well as their eyes. One was a mother who worried about what would happen to her dear girl if she did win and what would happen to their family if she didn't.

"The basics are complete. Now, it is time to show us what new steps you bring to our county," instructed Mr. McSorley. "Gran Ryan, begin your tally now."

Before the eyes of the crowd, the portly man and the young girl became dueling dancers, their pointing toes and rigid arms their weapons. O'Sullivan went first. His new steps were simple variations of the basics, created with minimal effort and danced with only passable skill.

Then it was Meggy's turn. Dan played his first notes, and

Meggy's feet froze. Everyone was waiting. She could feel their eyes burning holes in her shabby shoes. "I can't move me feet, let alone dance," she thought, desperate. But first Master Cleary caught her eye, then Mam, Fiona and Dan. The warmth of their belief in her melted her frozen feet and set her spirit free.

Her steps were totally original and breathtaking. Her light weight and strong legs allowed her to step high enough to have time for complicated moves like her Whirling Pivot and Heaven's Heelswing. Never had the crowd seen such a high level of difficulty.

Although Meggy's steps were far more original and difficult, it made no difference. The contest rules called for the greatest number of new steps. When Gran Ryan announced her count, they were tied.

Mr. McSorley asked, "Who can suggest a tie-breaker?"

O'Sullivan said, "Let's have a dance-off. The last one standing is the winner." He thought, "Miss Meggy's fancy footwork won't help her then. That half-starved child will never outlast a strong man like me, in the prime of my life."

But the crowd was shouting "NO DANCE OFF! NO DANCE OFF!" "It would take too long! There wouldn't be time for our dancin'!" "We came all this way to dance."

"Sorry, O'Sullivan," said Mr. McSorley. "Has anyone another idea?"

O'Sullivan would have objected strongly if he had known the identity of the work-worn but still beautiful woman who made the next suggestion. Looking at the crowd rather than her daughter she said, "A dance master must be a good teacher as well as a good dancer. Let each competitor choose eight children and teach them a new dance."

"A wise suggestion!" said Mr. McSorley. "Being able to teach is just as important as a master's ability to dance." The crowd clapped their agreement.

O'Sullivan's crafty mind was immediately busy. "Since Miss Meggy is little more than a child herself, let her teach the little ones," he suggested. "I will instruct the young ladies in an advanced set which only a master of my experience could handle."

Mr. McSorley replied sternly, "O'Sullivan, I hope your suggestion is only the result of speakin' before thinkin'. Otherwise, it appears that you are tryin' to cheat Miss Meggy out of a fair competition. Our young ladies have had a decade of lessons with Fancy Feet himself." He proposed the rules: "Each competitor will select eight children. When the sun touches the top of that oak, each group will be ready. Then we will vote for the best teacher."

Meggy sat on the ground with her chosen little ones. She asked, "Would you like to learn the Cherub's Jig?" Wide-eyed, they nodded *yes*. Meanwhile, stiff as a troop of soldiers, O'Sullivan's students stood in a straight line in front of his door-floor. "Isn't there one of you who knows your right foot from your left? Drop your bodyweight onto the right foot on count one, change of weight on counts two and three being significantly less," he ordered.

Not understanding the terms he used, the children became more nervous and made more and more mistakes. They fell over each other's feet and traipsed on each other's toes. They circled right when they should have circled left. The more mistakes they made the more he yelled. "You halfwits! You dunderheads! You morons!" Soon every child stood stock still, afraid to make a move.

Meggy's clear voice rang out merrily, "Turn to the couple on your left, form a tight circle…" Her pupils changed partners, just the way she taught them. The progress of Meggy's group made O'Sullivan furious. "Her little heathens are already dancin' in a circle. How did I get stuck with every Kerry child with two left feet? Well, I know just how to deal with that."

As the sun turned the last leaves on the oak, brilliant again, Mr. McSorley called, "Our two competitors will now demonstrate their teachin' skills. Who will be first?"

Looking nothing like the cocky man they had first met, O'Sullivan shook his head *no*. Definitely *no*. His ankles were as swollen as a cow's udder left unmilked. But Meggy's little dancers answered for her, "We will! We will! We want to be first!"

Proudly, she introduced them. "Me Kerry Angels will perform the Cherub's Jig." They danced with light feet and happy hearts. Their parents smiled with pride. Master Cleary understood how Meggy felt as she passed her joy on to her students. Mam felt pride and a tug of sadness, thinking, "If only Mac could be standin' proudly beside me."

Then it was O'Sullivan's turn. He barked out the steps. He and the hazel switch he had cut down from a nearby hedge had forced his pupils to learn. But not one child smiled. One little fella was crying. Mothers pointed to red welts on their childrens' legs. Angry fathers began to make their way to the front of the crowd.

No one ever knew what caused the accident. Perhaps the door was slippery with evening dew. Perhaps it was the flood of sweat streaming off O'Sullivan's drenched body. But suddenly he fell, so hard he cracked the door. Refusing Meggy's offer of a hand up, he struggled to his feet, his face red. Looking for someone else to blame, he roared like a bull who thinks he still owns the meadow, "Which of you brats soaped my door?" When no one answered, he became angrier still. "Then you Kerry folk are cheaters one and all, especially your darling Miss Meggy!"

The crowd was dangerously silent. Turning away, O'Sullivan yelled over his shoulder, "I'll never step foot in Kerry again."

"You'll have me to deal with if you do," threatened Roddy. "And me." "And me." "And me." added the fathers of children whose legs still stung from the man's switch.

Before he had even quite disappeared from sight, Dan whistled up some music. He was joined by the fiddler. The crossroads filled with dancers. The couples were husbands and wives, grannies and grandsons, sweethearts young and old. All responded to the calls. "Change places, chain and swing, all dancers step it out."

Dance of Life

Many lined up to dance with Meggy. For her there was only one partner, her beloved Master Cleary. Looking up into his gray eyes, she wished the reel would never end. With the magic of their dance still with her, she turned Roddy down to go look for Fiona. Finding her at the edge of the crowd, she whispered, "Can you believe he's here, Fiona—that he risked his life for me and me family—that I danced in his arms?"

Her best friend answered with a hug. "I'll not be spoilin' the magic of the night, by tellin' her that Master Cleary is even now slippin' away from us, back into hidin'," she thought.

The two girls joined a circle of laughing dancers and danced until dawn woke the sky. Roddy made sure he had the last dance. On the way home, Meggy MacGillycuddy, County Kerry's first female dance mistress, fell sound asleep in her mother's arms.

With his Meggy safe at home, Roddy led his uncles to the well. Peering down they saw the traitor clinging to the rope for dear life. Seamus was shivering so badly the bucket had splashed him soaking wet. 'There's the rat I told ye about," said Roddy.

"P-p-please. L-l-l-let m-m-me out," Fox begged between chatters. Roddy and his crew hauled Seamus up. But they did not untie him until they warned him what would happen if he spied on Meggy or any of their loved ones again. When they freed him, Seamus stumbled down the road, as fast as his shivering legs would take him.

Rumor had it thereafter that he remained so terrified of water he could not even sit in his own tub.

7

❖

night journeys

"Wake up! Wake up, Miss Meggy MacGillicuddy, County Kerry's first and only dance mistress!" crowed Dan again and again. Despite the late night he was awake earlier than usual. Meggy kept her eyes closed, hoping he would go away. Mam, who was also wishing for a few more minutes in their warm bed, felt Da stiffen and sit straight up. All of a sudden they realized the secret they had kept so carefully from him had now been told.

Sitting up, Mam saw Dan perched on the end of the bed, the realization of what he had done spreading with worry across his face. Meanwhile, his father, whose balance problems were much worse in the morning, was now staggering around the cottage.

So angry that his hand was shaking, her father held a paper in front of Meggy's sleep warm face. His fierce scribbled words startled her wide awake. *YOU—A DANCE MASTER??*

Looking desperately at her mother, she realized there were no right words to respond to this question. They had decided not to tell her father about the competition unless she won, neglecting to consider *how* they might tell him. Now he had found out in the worst way. He was so angry that his not-yet-well body was trembling from head to toe.

Afraid that his anger would make his illness worse, Mam tried to calm him. "We'll tell you the truth, Mac. But first come and sit in your chair."

He sat down reluctantly, looking from one face to another in angry expectation.

Meggy tried to hold his hand as she sat on the cold clay floor at his feet. But he yanked it away. She sighed, thinking, "Before the accident we sat and watched the fire like this every night. I want me old Da back. I want to be his darlin' Meggy again. But wantin' won't keep us from losin' our home. I have to try to make him understand." Looking up she said, "Da, we were afraid the worry of this terrible truth would keep you from gettin' well."

Taking the eviction notice from where it was hiding in the blanket box Mam held it out for him to read. Grabbing the paper, he crumpled it into a ball and threw it into the fire Dan was stirring. Sparks flew up too close to his small son's face.

His wife, who had been so patient, now spoke firmly, "Mac, burning it will not make our eviction go away. The rent must be paid and the truth is you are too sick to earn it. So Meggy must. You should be proud of her for winnin' this well payin' job."

Meggy added, "I tried to get a job here in the village. But Deirdre's old job at the pub went to Finbar's young widow, Nell." Taking a deep breath and looking right into her father's eyes she asked, "Da, now that you understand why, will you be givin' me your approval to work as a dance mistress?"

His face turned purple. His eyes bulged out as he slashed out his final answer.

OVER MY DEAD BODY

So without his approval, the other three went quietly about getting Meggy ready, hoping that in time Da would accept and understand. Others helped too. The villagers were proud of their Meggy. One gave a blanket for cold nights on the road, another a boy's cap and breeches for her disguise. Roddy would give her a lift when he could. Mr. McSorley gave her the names of good Irish folk who would take her in and watch out for her on her travels. Danny gave her his lucky stone from their crystal cave.

Her mother had cleverly fashioned a pack for her to carry her few belongings in. Made out of an old sack, it had straps so she could wear it on her back and still have her hands free. Folding up the two lace panels and rainbow of ribbons and placing her competition costume carefully inside, Meggy felt the magic of that night again.

Fiona gave one of her dear departed brother's belongings. Johnny had died for Ireland and now her best friend would wear his boots. Meggy knew how much Fiona and her mam cherished these last earthly bits of their much-loved brother and son. She was surprised his boots weren't way too big for her until she remembered that Johnny was only fourteen and far from his man-size when he was killed.

"Thank you Fiona, having Johnny's boots will keep me from completely wearin' out me already shoddy shoes and becoming a barefoot dance mistress," said Meggy, trying to tease the sadness of the moment away. In Fiona's world, Meggy and her dear departed brother were the only two who loved her. Her father loved only the poteen and her mother's love had died with Johnny. Her heart ached with the fear of losing Meggy, too. But she would not add her fears to the burdens her friend was already carrying. Kneeling down she gave her a hand in untangling a stubborn knot. That gave them both a chance to wipe away their tears.

Only one problem remained; telling her father. That evening, Mam asked, "Meggy come and stir the broth, me back is sore." She spoke in a voice lower than the bubbling of the kettle. "Darlin' girl, never tell your da about your job. He'll be forever angry. And anger makes his headaches worse."

"Mam, I must work as dance mistress. I must earn enough to pay our rent," Meggy replied.

"I have a plan," continued Mam. "But it means we have to lie to your father. We'll tell him that Aunt Tilly, with eight children already, has a sickly baby and needs your help."

Meggy sighed and nodded. "As much as I hate to leave on a lie, it's a good and necessary plan. Da won't mind me stayin' with his sister Tilly."

"I'll tell him when he wakes," Mam said "He and I will be alone then. You'll need to go around and tell the others about the lie. Then they won't be givin' us away when visitin'. Start at the pub and the well. Make sure you tell Dan first. He feels so bad about tellin' our first secret I know we can trust him with this one."

So two evenings later when her bag was packed, her disguise donned in the privy and the lie well told, County Kerry's newest dance mistress slipped as quiet as the bats above into the gathering dusk. On reaching the pubyard, Meggy hid behind the rain barrel until Mr. McSorley showed up. She knew it would not be long, because their donkey was harnessed to the loaded trap, ready to make their secret deliveries. Suddenly she felt a rush of air from behind her and then she was swooped up and dropped unceremoniously on the beast's back. Having been scared half to death, Meggy was just ready to unleash a volley of angry words at Roddy when his father appeared.

Giving her disguise a good look Mr. McSorley chuckled, "Well I thought it was the lovely Meggy MacGillycuddy who would be travellin' with us tonight. But it seems we have a young Mac MacGillycuddy instead."

Roddy graciously doffed his cap and said, "Miss Meggy-Mac MacGillycuddy, please meet Miss Bessie-Mae McSorley, the darlingest donkey you'll ever know and not nearly as stubborn as some girls I've known.

"Miss Bessie-Mae McSorley, please meet Miss Meggy-Mac MacGillycuddy, the darlingest dancer you'll ever know and more stubborn than most donkeys I've known."

Meggy was denied the pleasure of giving Roddy a good smack on his ever-yammering gob, because having never ridden a donkey before she was too terrified to let go. So she retaliated with her quick wit and sharp tongue. "How nice to meet you, Miss Bessie-Mae. I see now why Roddy is such an ass. With his lovely long ears and fine furry face, he definitely takes after your side of the family."

Roddy's father let out a snort of laughter. Then he made a clucking sound with his tongue and Miss Bessie-Mae toddled off, out of the village. Once Meggy got used to the donkey's rolling gait she rather liked the warm feel of its shaggy gray body beneath her. Not used to being out at night she was surprised by the dark blanket of quiet which had fallen over Kerry's gentle hills. She gasped at the beauty. "Look at the stars! They're so bright and the sky is so deeply dark, they look like diamonds on Queen Boadicea's blue silk tunic."

Roddy and his father walked beside the cart in silence. They had decided not to spoil Meggy's first magical ride by telling her of the merciless soldiers who could be waiting to ambush them 'round the next bend. From many midnight

journeys, their eyes had become keen in the dark. They kept a vigilant watch with every step they took.

Bessie-Mae's steady steps were lulling Meggy to sleep. But just when she was about to nod off, there would be a steep hill to climb or a wooden bridge for the donkey to clip-clop across. As the midnight hours crawled by, Meggy became more and more uncomfortable, but was too embarrassed to admit it. "Aren't they ever goin' to take a break? Now I know why they are walkin' and not ridin'. Each time we go over a bridge, it feels like every one of its boards and every one of Bessie's backbones is being applied directly to me bottom."

Noticing his guest squirming uncomfortably, Mr. McSorley declared himself in need of a cold drink and a bit of a sit. Roddy rushed to help her down, not wanting to miss an opportunity to get Meggy into his arms. Trying to avoid his all too friendly hands, Meggy slipped down herself. Her planned graceful dismount turned into a ragdoll tumble on the ground. Her legs were asleep.

With a great smirk on his face, Roddy slipped his arms under hers and stood Meggy back up, as he would a wee one learning to walk. She stomped off towards a burbling stream as fast as her pins-and-needles legs would go. "Meggy!" Roddy whispered, and pointed to a rocky shallow. Meggy saw a fox drop the fat goose he was carrying upon his back, and bend his neck to quench his thirst.

Meggy said quietly, "That sly fellow makes me think of Seamus. He spent so much time followin' me I worried he might learn about the competition and I would end up a prisoner of Lord Black's bullies. But then he disappeared. Have either of you seen him?"

McSorley Senior said, "Not I," with the confidence of a man with a clear conscience.

McSorley Junior did not have such a straightforward answer. "Rumor has it that Seamus dropped a coin in the well and was so determined to get it, he fell in. All were at the crossroads that night so no one came to his rescue till nearly dawn. Four fellows found him hangin' on to the bucket rope for dear life. Word is that when they pulled him up, Fox looked like a drowned rat. They say he was so cold you could hear his knees knockin'."

Meggy studied Roddy's face suspiciously. "How is it that you're knowin' so much about Seamus's unfortunate accident?"

Winking over her head at his father, Roddy answered, "You'll discover as you travel with us that at each stop we often receive a bit of news as well as our rightful payment."

Before she could ask more, the McSorley men got busy swishing the road dust out of their throats with the stream water. Taking a hankie from her pocket, Meggy wet it and wiped her face clean. Her skin, glowing pearly as the moon, took Roddy's breath away.

"What are you starin' at, ye big foolish eejit?" demanded Meggy.

"I'm just tryin' to look out for ye," replied Roddy. Then taking a bit of clay from the creek bank he smeared it across her pretty nose and said, "Meggy, if you want others to see you as a lad, it would be wise to be keepin' your beauty hiding under some dirt."

Before she could grab a chunk of clay to return the favor, Mr. McSorley said, "You know, Meggy, I think me son is right this time. Your face has grown too beautiful by far to ever be mistaken for a boy's. You'd best do as he says."

So with a sore bottom, hurt pride and clay smeared all over her face Meggy turned and walked determinedly off down the road. Her patience could no more bear another minute of the know-it-all grin on Roddy's face than her bottom could bear another minute on Bessie-Mae's bony back. Wise Mr. McSorley laid a hand on his son's arm and shook his head when Roddy started after her.

It wasn't till after two hours of steady walking with the McSorley's behind her that the song of a lark made Meggy aware of the beauty of the awakening countryside. The green swathes of pastureland were a lovely background for sleeping chestnut-brown mares and their colts. From higher up came the bleat of a lamb, probably nuzzling its mother for breakfast. The dawn wiped clean Meggy's anger and filled her with peace.

Mr. McSorley, who had stepped up beside her, heard her stomach grumble and said, "Meggy, would you believe that griddle cakes are bein' cooked for us just around the bend, in Finfaerie. The Griffins will be the first family to have the honor of sharin' their home with ye. Their children will take you to their secret school, where you, Miss Meggy, County Kerry's first female dance mistress, will conduct your first official lessons." Then the kindly man instructed her on the best route and safest places to call.

The Griffins welcomed them warmly, the Griffin children watching Meggy curiously as she and the McSorleys ate. After breakfast Mr. McSorley drew her to him for a warm goodbye hug. Roddy, trying to hide the sudden fear he felt at the prospect of leaving her behind, asked, "And what about me, Miss Meggy? Surely you'll need a kiss to be remembering me by?" Before she had time to say no he stepped closer and leaned down. But instead of giving her a kiss and a hug he ended up cracking her head and treading on her toes.

"Thanks for the memories, Roddy," said Meggy, trying not to join the giggles of the Griffin children behind her.

8

❖

DANCING FOR A LIVING

Holding hands, Meggy and the Griffin children ran along paths, over streams and down green hills. They made a pretty picture for anyone watching. Seven red-headed children sized like stairsteps, from Philip the oldest at 13, to Marie-Therese in the middle at ten, down to dear little Dermot, all trying to catch the attention of their lovely raven-haired visitor. All anyone could wish for them would be that only friendly eyes were watching.

Meggy had not had such fun since before the soldiers came, when she and Dan ran through the woods, tipping toadstools and chasing butterflies. The Griffin children led her to their temporary hedgeschool. Their last one had been destroyed only three weeks before. She watched as they disappeared, one by one, behind a large rock at the edge of a field. Philip led the way and Marie-Therese brought up the rear. Meggy had no choice but to follow. Behind the first growth, the villagers had cleverly created a maze, twisting and turning through the tallest field of hogweed she had ever seen. Following the path, she was entirely surrounded in a secret world of green-gold stalks and the blue of a Kerry sky. The children were waiting in the center clearing that was, for now, their hedgeschool.

Looking back, Mistress Meggy laughed, "It's lucky I've all of you to be leadin' me out of this field of confusion. Otherwise I would likely be so lost I'd have to be spendin' the night." Inside the warm protection of the maze and its green-growing walls, Meggy felt safe. She made their lessons such fun that not one had time to think about making mischief.

They told her of another dance master, who had taught them lessons for two days.

"Why only two days?" asked Meggy, hoping another teacher had not met a fate as terrible as Fancy Feet's.

The children looked at each other and then at Marie-Therese, their oldest sister. She spoke for the rest of them. "When our da and some of the other fathers saw the marks of the switchin's that man gave us, they chased him out of town." She pulled up the raggedy leg of her littlest brother's pants. "This wound is three months old. That cruel man switched our wee Dermot again and again, just because he did not yet know his right foot from his left."

Meggy gasped in horror. The red and still-festering welt

went from the back of the poor little fellow's knee all the way down to his ankle. Now she knew why he was so timid.

"Our fathers chased that bully right out of town. When he saw the big switches they were carryin', the coward was terrified he'd be receivin' what he'd so cruelly given."

Philip added bluntly, "He was puffin' and pantin', his big belly hangin' out, all the while beggin' for his wages. He got exactly what he deserved—absolutely nothin'!"

Then wee Dermot peeked out from behind his sister's skirt and shyly added, "And he wasn't pretty like you, Miss Meggy," before hiding again.

The dear little fellow reminded her so much of Dan that Meggy experienced her first tug of homesickness. Curiosity made her ask, "Did this man wear a cloak of many colors?"

"Yes, yes!" answered the children.

"His name was John James O'Sullivan," added Marie-Therese. "Do you know him?"

Her suspicions confirmed, Meggy replied simply, "Only in passin', only in passin'."

To herself, she hoped never to see the horrid man again. But a niggle of fear told Meggy she must always be on the lookout for him.

Each day brought more and more children to Miss Meggy's dance school. As Friday—pay day—drew near, twenty-one students made up her class. Before falling asleep Thursday night she calculated that she could earn forty-two pence at two pence per student.

"If I earn that much each week, I'll be able to go home and pay the rent well before Christmas." She fell asleep to dream of a sweet homecoming and a pack full of coins.

When lessons were done, Marie-Therese came first to drop the Griffins' coins, a child's worth at a time, into her lap. Meggy had hoped for more, but they did share their home and meals with her. She had to bite her tongue at the measly amount that came from a family of four, not even enough for one student. To keep her from complaining, the next family had sent their payment with the smallest child. Checking their names off, she said a polite thank-you. And so it went.

That night, on her straw bed in the loft, Meggy counted and recounted the coins. Not once did it come anywhere near what she needed to earn in a week. She worried, "I must do better, but how? Are they payin' me less because I'm a girl?"

Lying back, she remembered listening to Master Cleary talking after he had joined them for a meal. She remembered her da apologizing when the payments had been small, and offering to take the master down to the pub to earn a few coins by writing letters for those that couldn't. The master quickly accepted.

"I must find a way to let the villagers know I could write for them," Meggy decided. Searching through her scrap papers, she chose the biggest and the best. But not owning a pen, she would have to wait till morning to borrow the

Griffins'. She fell asleep planning the notice that would announce her abilities as a scribe.

Next morning she dressed in the dark and waited until she heard Mrs.Griffin wake the fire. Used to being alone that early, the good woman was startled to see her guest's long legs emerge from the loft. Meggy asked to borrow their pen and then sat at the table to write. "Now if I can just get this written perfectly, before those seven ever-jigglin', ever-spillin' children join me," she sighed.

Good men and women of Finfaerie, do you have requests to be written, love letters to be answered, poems to be penned?

If so I will write any missive you need for a modest fee. I guarantee the proper spelling and fine penmanship, taught to me by Master Timothy Cleary himself.

Meggy waited politely till Mr. Griffin finished his breakfast. "Sir, ye have been so kind in sharin' your home with me. I feel that I should not be askin' ye yet another favor."

"Miss Meggy, the pleasure is all ours," Mr. Griffin assured her. "You've set not only our children's feet, but also their hearts a dancin'. Now what is it you need?"

Cheeks red with embarrassment, Meggy spoke the hard-told truth. "You know me wages are to keep me family from bein' evicted. But me dance classes are not earnin' near the coin I need. Would you post this notice at the pub, where all can see I will work as a scribe?"

"That is not a favor, Miss Meggy. Your writin' skills will be a service to many. But I'll not post your notice as it might be read by enemy eyes. Instead I'll pass it from one Irish hand to another. I'll also spread the word as there are those who can't read. You were wise not to sign your name. That way anyone who seeks your services will have to go through me. I'll make sure there are no informers in the lot."

Mrs. Griffin, who had managed to catch most of their conversation above the chatter of her children, put her arm around Meggy's shoulder. "You could be earnin' more by teachin' adults, too. Let's invite a few couples around Saturday night for a class. They'd enjoy learnin' some of your original steps and dances which I've seen the little ones practicin' out back."

Laughing, Mr. Griffin put his arm around his wife's waist. "Well, isn't herself just as bright as the sunshine this mornin'? That's a fine idea. It's been too long since we had a ceilidh."

Meggy's face glowed with hope but fear niggled at her mind. "Are ye not afraid informers or soldiers may find out? I could not bear to have your cottage torched or your children put at risk because of me."

Mr. Griffin said, "Don't you be worryin'. We just ran our last traitor out of town. We're always watchin'. If we smell trouble brewin' we'll put the ceilidh off a bit."

Accepting his reassurance, Meggy sighed. She had forgotten how safe it felt to be able to depend on your da for help.

Of course when the Griffin children heard of the ceilidh they insisted on attending. And if they were attending, then so must their friends. If their friends were comin' then so must their cousins. And their cousins couldn't attend without the aunts and uncles. If they were invitin' the aunts and uncles then the grannies must come too.

When that special Saturday night and the guests arrived, Meggy peeked down from her loft. It seemed all in the village and all their relatives had come. There was even a black-faced lamb bunting the guests' hands, hoping for a head rub. She worried, "How can I be teachin' a dance lesson if there is not even room for me two feet on the floor?"

Noticing her, Mrs. Griffin called, "Come down, Meggy. We can't begin without ye."

"I'll be right there," she replied. But her stomach was doing such a jig of its own she had to sit down. "Teachin' children is one thing, but facin' a cottage full of adults is another. One look at me, a young and shabby female, and they'll decide I couldn't possibly be a dance mistress of any worth!" Kicking her pack hard, she added, "And they just might be right."

When the pack tipped over, a spill of ribbons fell onto the floor. Reaching to pick them up, Meggy thought, "Well, I'll at least feel more presentable if I tie me mop of curls back with one of these." But when she tugged on the ribbons she got more than she counted on. Her mother had carefully tied the ribbons to one sleeve of her white tunic. After pulling out the rest of her competition costume, it took Meggy but a moment to decide this was just what she needed for her debut performance in Finfaerie.

Embarrassed to have her bottom be the first thing those below would view of her she climbed down as gracefully as possible.

Taking her hand, Mr. Griffin bowed to her. Then turning to his guests he said, "Please welcome Miss Meggy, County Kerry's first dance mistress." Even those not sure about a female dance instructor were curious to see one who was bold enough to try.

"Show us what ye can do, Dance Mistress Meggy," demanded one of those loud voices that always come from the back, where no one can be sure who the speaker is.

Meggy, who had planned on teaching a class first, was caught off guard. The Griffin children came to her rescue. "Do that dance you do when you think no one is watchin'," they suggested. "The one you have the music in your head for."

Before she could even agree, Mr. Griffin was moving the crowd, "Step back, step back—give the dance mistress some room."

And then in came Philip, the top half of their door held over his head. "There you go, Miss Meggy—now you've got your own dance floor."

With all eyes on her, Meggy knew there was no turning back. Giving the Griffins a charming curtsy she took her position on the door-floor. The music that was always in her heart did not desert her. From the first arched point of her toe and the first graceful lift of her arm, she captured the attention of each and everyone. Even her critics forgot that the dancer was female, young and inexperienced. The more she felt them with her, the faster her toes tapped, the higher her legs leapt. Astonished to see her do such high leaps and fast twirls on such a small dance floor, one man gasped, "Why, that girl could dance a jig on a plate!"

As her feet brushed, clicked, shuffled and tipped, Meggy knew she was doing what she was meant to do. "Now if I can just earn enough doin' it, all will be fine come Christmas."

The dance class had so many interested students that their mistress had to move between three sets of eight dancers. All it took from her was the straightening of a leg here and a quick reteaching of a swing there. Meggy made the learning so easy that no one could say when the lesson had ended and the fun had begun.

The ceilidh was successful also for the business arrangements that resulted. On Monday evening Mr. Griffin escorted Meggy to the pub. There she listened and wrote carefully as the villagers trusted her with their most private thoughts—the love for a sweetheart far away; the fear for a son gone too long; the anger of a brother swindled.

In thanks, she gave Mr. and Mrs. Griffin a private class that night. The partnership between husband and wife made her teaching easy. When they had learned all they needed from her, she slipped up to the loft. Lying on her bed, listening to their soft laughter, Meggy couldn't help but wish. "Oh, what I'd give to see Da dancin' Mam around our cottage again, to see them so taken up with each other that they forget Dan and I are peekin' at them from the bed."

The peace of her nights in the loft and the joy of days spent dancing made Meggy feel suddenly guilty. "It is so easy to forget how sick Da is and how hard it must be for Dan and Mam." Away from the reality, she could almost believe that when she got back the angry man would have disappeared forever, that her dear da would be waiting with open arms.

From the minute she woke up the next morning, Meggy began a whirl of days spent in classes with the children and evenings spent writing at the pub. When the Thursday of the third week arrived, she was enjoying a rare night off. The children were roasting chestnuts and young Dermot was giving her poor tired feet a rub. The sweet smell of the peat fire and the gentle massage lulled her into a half sleep.

She awoke when Philip whispered in her ear, "Would ye like to be slippin' away tomorrow night with Marie-Therese, meself and our friends? They will bring torches and we will be able to spend the night dancin' under the stars."

Her blistered feet might have disagreed, but the idea was tempting. "Will I be goin' as dance mistress or just as Meggy?" she asked.

"You won't be teachin' a single lesson, only dancin' for the fun of it," Philip promised.

"Well then, not even St. Patrick's snakes could be keepin' me away!" she replied. A little fun, with people her own age, was just what Meggy needed. She was sorely missing Fiona and perhaps even Roddy too, not that she would ever admit it.

Philip cautioned, "It must be kept secret because we don't want the little ones taggin' along. Besides Mam and Da wouldn't let us go for fear that soldiers might capture us."

Remembering her own too-close calls Meggy asked, "Will we be safe, Philip?"

His face turned serious, "As safe as an Irish Catholic can be. We'll post two lookouts. If anyone approaches we'll douse the torches and sneak off through the hogweed. There is not an Englishman alive who could find his way through our maze, in the dark of a Kerry night."

So the next evening after putting on her other dress, and tying her tumble of black curls back with a red ribbon, she was ready for some fun. The minute they saw the torches, Philip let out a wild howl and raced into the field. Meggy felt a thrill of adventure lick the hairs on the back of her neck as she joined the others running like a long and laughing snake through the maze. At the center, the fellows shoved the torches into the ground. One brought out his tin whistle and the dancing began.

Only in hiding places by the lake had Meggy ever danced with such abandon. The dancers and the music had become one. They appeared and disappeared like strange fairies. Their whirling sets led them into the circles of torchlight and out again. Two-by-two shadows stretched into giants and giantesses leaping from corner to corner. Then, in the middle, the shadows hunched and squatted, like the magic ones deciding who to share their power with.

Meggy and the other girls shrieked like banshees as their partners swung them faster and faster, higher and higher. Meggy's mind whirled with images. "With the torchlight shadowin' their faces and dazzling their eyes, the others look like changelin's, caught between life as mortals or fairies. What would a mirror show me of meself?" she wondered.

The wind wailed, like a fairy mistress rejected by the mortal partners dancing just out of her reach. Then like a lover scorned it blew out three of the torches, leaving the dancers suddenly still. Like good Kerry folk, no one questioned the message of the wind. It was time to take up one still-burning torch and follow it now, through the maze and home.

Meggy stared at the torchlight. The white heat at its center seared the magic of the night into her memory forever.

The next day, even damper and colder than usual, found most of the Griffins inside their small cottage. Tired from last night's wild dancing, Meggy, like Philip and Marie-Therese, sat staring into the fire, oblivious to the constant noise of the other children.

Meggy jerked awake, sure she had seen Danny calling to her from the flames. But that frightened little voice was young Dermot's. "I was makin' mulberry mud pies behind the bush, when I heard a carriage comin'. I knew by the two

black horses that used to be ours that it was Lord Power. But he was not alone. The bad man was with him!"

Squatting down beside him, Meggy asked, "What bad man, Dermot?"

"This bad man,"answered the frightened little fella, yanking up his pants leg.

Philip stepped forward. "Do ye mean that bully of a dance master, O'Sullivan?"

Dermot nodded yes. His father's face flushed red. "Why would he dare come back?"

His mother asked, "Dermot, did you see which way the carriage went?"

"Yes" he said, "but first it stopped."

Taking a deep shuddering breath Meggy asked, "What happened then?"

Looking into her eyes, the boy said, "The bad man pointed at our cottage. He said, 'She's there. My informer told me that family is hidin' a law-breakin' dance mistress.' Then Lord Power said he would send for soldiers to, to, to torch our roof and capture..."

No one needed him to finish the sentence. Sniffing and wiping his tears, he continued, "He held a whip and he kept c- c- crackin' it and crackin' it again and again. He s-s-said, 'It's been too long since I've had the pleasure of whippin' a pretty girl.'" Dermot sobbed and sobbed while repeating over and over, "I'm sorry, Meggy. I'm sorry."

Shoving her own fear aside, Meggy comforted him. "Dermot

you were so brave to stay there and listen to those scary men. Now I have time to pack, while your family gets rid of any evidence of me stay. You may have saved your cottage *and* me."

She raced up the steps to gather her belongings. Marie-Therese followed. Spotting the boy's clothing her friend said, "You'd best wear these."

Meggy tore her dress off and jumped into the pants and boots. Marie-Therese rolled her friend's precious coins into the discarded dress and tied the bundle tightly with the sleeves. Then she helped her friend pull on the shirt and stuff her black curls under the cap. The rest of the family had searched their cottage for any traces of their guest—a red ribbon, a letter written in her hand. Mr. Griffin and Philip stood guard at the door.

Hearing the pounding of horses' hooves, Meggy (now Mac) ran out the door. She slipped around the corner of the cottage and into the dusk.

Meggy had barely passed the privy when she heard the horses stop and the sound of angry voices. As she could not stay to listen, she prayed as she ran, "Please, please let me friends be spared. Let their cottage remain untorched and their family unhurt."

By pretending not to understand English, Mr. Griffin and Philip kept the landlord, his bullies and the traitorous O'Sullivan at the door as long as possible. When they finally stormed in, the children and their mother were at the table, innocently winding skeins of yarn.

The big angry men filled the cottage. They turned over the family's few bits of furniture and smashed a pair of cherished cups. Flipping open the settle bed they jabbed their bayonets into the tangle of blankets. Spotting the loft they raced up, howling with premature success. They found nothing there, nothing but straw.

The Griffin family faced question after question. Each time they answered, "No milord. Not here milord," their landlord cracked his whip harder and faster against his glove. He began to look with anger at O'Sullivan, who had led him on this wild goose chase.

Still not having learned when to keep his mouth shut, O'Sullivan whined, "I beg you to believe me, your lordship. She *must* be here. I know she must."

Lord Power cracked the whip in the blabbering bully's direction and strode away. He and his soldiers thundered out of the village, not noticing the lad who had to jump into a hawthorn hedge to get out of their way. It was a good thing, too, because the tumble dislodged his cap to display a beautiful head of long raven curls.

9

❖

ЭАПGER İП ᴄᴅE ЭARK

She lay in the hedge till the last hoofbeat of hard-run horses disappeared. Trying to get up, Meggy realized she was held back by thorns that tied her hair to the hedge as tightly as Lord Power might have tied her to his whipping post. Scared, frustrated, and alone, she pulled and pulled till a big chunk of her hair tore right out from the roots. She could barely hold back a scream. More boys than she could count had pulled her tumble of black curls but not all their tugs together could have hurt that much.

The brave Dance Mistress MacGillycuddy dissolved into the fourteen-year-old girl she was and sobbed, "Oh, what I would give to be a little girl again. To have Mam here to coax the tangles out of me hair." As pictures of home flooded her memories, she could almost feel her mother's strong but gentle fingers working out the knots that tied themselves into her curls. "When I got impatient Mam would always say, 'Slow but sure, me darlin', slow but sure.'"

Taking a deep breath, Meggy pulled herself up till there was the least amount of pull on her hair. Reaching back she began to slowly unravel each silken curl from the gnarly grasp of the hedge. Her arms and shoulders ached long before she was done. By the time the last strand was untangled, the night was as black as her hair.

This dark was nowhere as exciting as the dark spent dancing in the maze with her friends. It was nowhere as beautiful as the starry night she had shared with Roddy and his da. "This dark is so empty, so complete. It leaves me cold and blind," shivered Meggy, glad for the company of her own voice. Standing up she brushed the dry leaves and dirt from her clothing. "Well, at least if it hides even the stars, perhaps it will hide me, too."

Worried about what might have fallen out, she pulled her pack off. "Oh, no, the flap is open." The dark inside was as deep as the night dark around her. Reaching in, Meggy used her fingertips to see what was there. She felt the warmth of the blanket, the lace and ribbons of her tunic, but not her dress. "Me dress has to be here," she said, searching frantically. "There it is!" she sighed and pulled it out. But this dress was not tied in a knot. This dress held no coins.

She didn't want to dump everything out, for fear of not

finding things again in the dark. "But I must," she told herself, with not even the moon to talk to. Sitting crosslegged, she pulled out one item at a time and put it in her lap. The closer she came to the bottom, the faster her heart pounded. Finally her hand felt the still knotted dress. "Now, if only all me coins are still there."

With shaking fingers she undid the knots. They were all there, along with something furry that wriggled scritchy, scratchy claws onto her hand. Later Meggy would wonder why she had not thrown the dress and coins off into the dark. Perhaps she sensed that the palm-sized creature was afraid, so afraid it was frozen in its spot. Cupping her surprise guest in her hands, she said, "It's all right, little wood mouse. You scared me, too. What are you doin' in me pack? Is that a wee crumb on your whisker?"

The little creature blinked in reply. "Could that be a bit of potato scone I see?" Reaching into the pack, she found the scone and a bit of black pudding too. Copying the twitchy sniffy movements of his nose, she pretended to scold, "Who's been nibbling my food?"

"What a fine hostess Mrs. Griffin was, thinkin' of me even when her home and family were in danger." Meggy smiled. "She must have tucked these in when we hugged goodbye.

"Well, Woody Woodmouse, since you found me food, it's only fair that I share it with ye. As you're not even as long as me hand and half that is tail, you won't be eatin' much. I'm all alone and not much likin' it, how would you like to travel along with me?"

The mouse tilted its head at her and scooted back into the pack.

"I guess that means yes," said Meggy. Feeling a little less alone, she carefully tucked the flap in and pulled the straps on, then headed down the black road to Drumaderry.

Woody was a tiny perfect travelling companion. Used to being up and about at night, he sat willingly on his new friend's shoulder, listening to her troubles and tales for the price of a few crumbs.

As the road and the night went on, Meggy became so tired that her booted feet felt like they had turned to stone. "If not for the betrayin' mouth and traitorous heart of O'Sullivan, I would not be walkin' alone in the dark. Just two more days at the Griffins and I would have been ridin' Bessie-Mae and Mr. McSorley would have been keepin' watch, keepin' us safe. Now when he comes to get me, no one will even know where I am. No one will know if the soldiers captured me." With a shudder she realized, "No one will know if I'm dead or alive."

Then just over the next rise, the faintest pink of morning showed her a scattering of dark little boxes. Gradually the rising sun painted them white and shone its yellow rays on the thatched roofs. When the fourth cottage past the well appeared, it was more beautiful than Mr. Mc Sorley could ever have described it.

After her long night's journey, Meggy was so happy to arrive at the Dunne's home, she forgot she had brought along an extra guest. When Woody scurried up the table leg to perch on her shoulder and share her breakfast, their startled hostess jumped up so quickly she knocked over her chair. Jumping up to help, she said, "I'm so sorry, Mrs. Dunne. Please let me explain." The bits and pieces of Woody's and Meggy's friendship came tumbling out before the lady of the house had a chance to order the both of them out.

Although Mrs. Dunne believed cleanliness was next to godliness (and that definitely didn't include a mouse in the house) she also had a kind heart. Looking at her own two daughters, sitting like blond bookends on either side of Meggy, she began to understand how much comfort a wee mouse could be on the dark and dangerous roads.

"You may stay, Meggy. But the mouse cannot," said her hostess.

Meggy promised, "I'll not be bringin' Woody in again." Later, she went to the shed where she had left her little friend. When she opened the door, he crept out to meet her in the pool of light that streamed in. "Woody, I promise to bring you lots of lovely nibbles, but you must stay here." It seemed as if the tiny fellow understood, because Mrs. Dunne never saw even a whisker of him again. Dragon, the Dunne's mean and massive cat who slept by the door all day, may also have influenced his decision.

Even though she had reached Drumaderry safely, Meggy's

walking was not done. She and the Dunne children had to walk for an hour down a hiding path to a dark and abandoned beehive hut. In times gone by, priests had held secret masses there and now the ancient stone shelter was the only place the villagers felt safe bringing their children.

Even then Meggy heard one mother say to another, "Do you think there is anywhere our children can be truly safe?"

The other answered, "If one more child disappears, I'm sendin' mine east to a second cousin. Even if they have to pretend to be Protestant it's better than havin' them dead."

Maybe it was the fear. Maybe it was the cold. Maybe it was the bleak shelter. But try as she might, Meggy had to struggle to bring the joy of dancing to Drumaderry. She thought, "The children's ears seemed more tuned to the hateful sound of the landlord's carriage or his soldiers' horses than the music. I see some signs they have not always been this way. One boy plays his penny whistle as well as Dan and another beats out a fine rhythm on the boudrain." Once two girls took off into a swirl of swinging dresses and then suddenly lost their concentration, as if Death himself had stepped between them. Miss Meggy sighed, "If only I could show them that escapin' into the dancin' is better than bein' swallowed up by the fear."

Counting up her second week's earnings, she realized that at least the parents were appreciating her efforts. "There is as much here as I earned in my whole time in Finfaerie. Perhaps I'll ask the parents to be their children's partners in a Sunday afternoon dance class."

After announcing the special class, Miss Meggy noticed small changes. Tiny toes tapped more vigorously. Little legs leapt higher. The odd smile flickered from one small face to another as the children circled round and round. Then from a tumble of two girls twirling too fast came a giggle, and then another and another, until the stone walls echoed with it. Their dance mistress didn't mind their wild laughter. In fact, as 'twas told over her students' dinner tables, "Miss Meggy laughed the hardest. Her laughin' is almost as beautiful as her dancin'."

Each day, more and more children arrived. Some walked for two hours just to be taught the dancing by kind and talented Dance Mistress Meggy.

That Sunday afternoon the stone hut hummed with activity. Spilling outside onto the pebbly ground, the children and their parents danced together for the first time since as long as they could remember. Two hours of dancing put color in their cheeks and light into their eyes. Stopping to watch, Miss Meggy's heart filled with joy.

The families walked home through the early dusk, holding hands and feeling something like hope in their hearts. The Dunne children all wanted to sleep beside Miss Meggy. Their father settled the argument by having them draw straws. Two slept on either side of her, with a promise to switch in the night. The fifth lay across the bottom of the bed. Their small hands and feet were icy cold against her but the smiles on their sleeping faces warmed their dance mistress as no blanket ever could.

As the Dunnes' cottage was set up on a bit of a ridge, they could see for miles around. Meggy took to sitting on the low branch of an oak tree to watch the stars. It was a peaceful way to end her day. Mr. Dunne had pointed out the direction of Copperkin, the beehive hut and Hag's Hollow, where she and Woody would travel next. Each night, she liked to look back toward home and send her love to her family. Then she would look ahead to Hag's Hollow, and wish for safety and new friends.

One night she saw something unusual. "What's that?" she wondered. "It looks like a giant red-gold snake headin' this way." Meggy's urgent call for Mr. Dunne also brought all the children to her ridge-top perch. Their eyes turned wide as they followed her pointing finger. Not one asked a question. They had all seen that flaming serpent before. They knew it devoured cottages, churches, homes, and hopes. "Soldiers," Mr. Dunne told Meggy, "Soldiers with torches."

As they watched, the snake seemed to break off into several fast-moving sections, all circling back in on them. The Dunnes ran inside to douse every candle, hoping their cottage would disappear into the dark and away from the soldiers' notice.

Mrs. Dunne rushed to collect the family's most treasured possesions. "You must go now," she said, passing Meggy her pack and her set of boy's clothes. Mr. Dunne handed Meggy all the coins he had. Then he placed his hands on her shoulders. "Meggy, let the stars guide you. They, not the soldiers, know where you're goin'." Led by the eldest, the children climbed down the far side of the ridge to a small cave. There, they and their parents would wait until the flames of the soldiers' anger had burnt out.

The thought of that flaming serpent sent Meggy racing first to the shed for Woody and then down the lane to a thick stand of oaks. There, panting and puffing, she changed from being Meggy to Mac. She hated to be moving again. "I wasn't here long enough to earn any writin' money. Me first appointments were to be tomorrow night." Hefting her tied-dress coin sack, she sighed, "They were payin' me so well. Many fathers gave me extra coins after our Sunday class. I could have earned a lot more if only I could have stayed a little longer."

Suddenly, the shame of her selfishness made Meggy look back to the home of her hosts. Thankfully there were no flames as big as the thatched roof of a burning cottage. She could not help but ask herself, "How many more times can I endanger the lives of other families in me quest to save me own?" Dropping to her knees she prayed for the survival of the Dunnes.

Meggy reached into her pack for her disguise, checking its contents and her small companion. The mouse had survived the wild run. Dressed once again as a boy, she sighed and said, "Well, Woody, it's just you and me, on the road again."

Meggy checked both ways. Not wanting to be caught by surprise again, she put her ear to the road to listen for hoof-beats. "Thank goodness for Mr. Dunne's starry roadmap, as I'm without a ride or a guide again. Will I ever be able to take up Mr. McSorley's kind offer?" The night was long but peaceful. Not a horse or donkey came Meggy's way. No soldiers, or informers passed by to observe, with evil curiosity, the slight youth traveling alone in the dead of night. When the moon showed her Hag's Hollow, settled into a foggy glen, she suffered no more than blistered feet and hunger pangs.

Even though it had been two months, Meggy remembered every bit Mr. McSorley had told her about the people who would take her in and where they lived. She especially remembered him speaking fondly of his Aunt Jessie, who smoked a pipe and would welcome her with fresh-baked honey cakes. Hers was the first cottage at the edge of town. Spotting a narrow track Meggy followed it up and around a stand of birch. From there she could see a cottage. As she got closer she could see the thatched roof had as many holes as her brother Dan had freckles. Surprised, she thought, "This is not what I expected. The walls are so dark and dirty it's hard to believe they were ever washed-white." Stopping to think, Meggy looked up at the sky and realized there were probably still two hours until dawn. "I can't be wakin' up an old woman this early. I'll just sit here on the step and rest me back on the door until I hear wakin' sounds inside."

So tired she was, Meggy fell asleep within minutes. What she didn't know was that the doorlatch was also in disrepair. The next thing she knew, she was flat on her back on a dirty floor, with an equally dirty man standing over her. He was as dark and unwelcoming as the place. "Who are ye and what are you doin' bargin' in here, in the middle of the night?"

One desperate look around the dark room told Meggy there would be no kind Aunt Jessie to welcome her. Feeling vulnerable, she grabbed her cap and struggled to get up. The man let her get to a sitting position before shoving a stinking foot on her head, to stop her from standing.

"Obviously I'm in the wrong house. I must apologize," thought Meggy. Looking up earnestly she said, "It's sorry I am to have disturbed your sleep. I've made a mistake and come to the wrong house. Please accept me apologies and I'll be leavin' you to your rest."

Again the man prevented her from standing. "I said, who are ye?"

Wanting to do whatever was needed to get away from him, Meggy answered in her most stern and official voice, "I'm Dance Mistress Meggy. The leaders of your village are awaiting me as we speak. They will come looking for me if I do not show up."

An angry female voice called from the bed, "Shut that door, ye fool. You're lettin' in the cold." Without showing a face, the voice spoke to Meggy, "We sent McSorley a message tellin' him we didn't want ye."

Stunned by the rudeness, Meggy said, "I was to be stayin with Mr. McSorley's Aunt Jessie, who makes honey cakes."

The man laughed sarcastically. "Well, ye sure won't be gettin' any honey cakes here. You can stay with Aunt Jessie, but you'll have to dig your own hole. We buried her in a pauper's grave nearly a year ago."

"That's a good one, Paddy," cackled the woman, who was now a set of bare, bony arms and a head topped with a rat's nest of dirty hair, sticking out from the soiled blanket.

While the dirty pair laughed at the sick joke, Meggy got to her feet. Her fear was giving way to anger. Boldly she asked, "Who are *you* and why are *you* livin' here?"

"Let's just say we were in the right place at the right time, weren't we, Gracie? Just in time to help the sick old hag hold her pen and sign the paper," snickered the man.

Meggy imagined the terrible way Mr. McSorley's poor Aunt Jessie had probably spent her last days, in the care of these two cold-hearted vultures. She turned to leave.

"Paddy, don't let her leave. Now that she's here, perhaps we can gain something out of it. Everyone fusses over the dance master, or should I say dance mistress? They'll be bringin' fine food for our honored guest. Plus, when they pay her, she'll pay us," plotted the lazy woman, who still had not sat up in bed.

Meggy's mind reeled. "I can't be stayin' here with these two." But when she tried to pull away from the man's grip, she heard a small voice say, "Please stay."

A bone-thin little girl had crawled up from under the cover at the end of the bed. She seemed all dark hair and big blue eyes, set into a small pale face. Meggy stared in wonder. "Jesus, Mary and Joseph! How could a child that beautiful have come from those two?"

"Please stay," the girl asked again, sweetly. "I'm lonely and I want to learn to dance."

The man yelled, "Shut up, brat! We don't have money for food, let alone dance lessons."

"Shut your own gob, Paddy. If the dance mistress stays here we'll make sure Annie gets free lessons," said Gracie, whose brain was the only thing about her that wasn't lazy.

"Yer a right smart one, aren't ye," said Paddy, leaning over and laying a slobbery kiss on her toothless mouth. "That's a fine idea. The best part is, with your whiny brat away with Mistress Meggy, we won't have to get out of bed all day."

"Those two have no room in their hearts or home for that dear little girl, let alone me." Preparing to run for it, Meggy took one last look around the room. That look did her in. The little girl held her arms out to Meggy. "Please stay. I'll carry in the peat and wake the fire. I'll make you mush for breakfast."

"Poor little Annie! She can't be more than five," Meggy thought. "Someone should be makin' breakfast for her." Next thing she knew the little girl was in her arms. It would have taken someone with a heart much harder than Meggy's to abandon the darling little child with the sad blue eyes.

10

❖

hAG'S hOLLOW

At first light the two raven-haired girls, one tall, one small, left the horrible excuse for a home. Neither adult so much as lifted a head to find out where the older girl, a stranger till an hour ago, was taking their small child.

Meggy was filled with worries. Usually they were about where she would teach and whether the villagers would like her or not. But that morning she kept asking herself, "What shall I do? I can't stay with those awful people for one night, let alone three or four weeks. But how can I leave Annie there, alone and uncared for?"

Annie pointed out the well and pulled her new friend towards the mothers and children there. Somehow they weren't surprised to see to Meggy. Word of her work was traveling around Kerry faster than she. Once the first child pointed out her presence, the rest ran to greet her. They formed a chattering circle of questions. "Are you the new dance mistress? Why are you here so soon? When do we start our lessons? When will we start? Will you come to our house for dinner? Will you come and stay with us?"

That last question brought the so far silent Annie out from behind her new friend's skirt. "Miss Meggy is stayin' with me." Her words shocked the small crowd to silence. The children stared at the little girl, whose clothes were not only tattered and too small, but dirty too. The mothers looked at one another with questions and concerns in their eyes.

Too young to be tactful, one lad said what all were thinking. "Annie, your cottage is dirty. The roof leaks. Your cupboards are bare. The dance mistress can't stay with you!"

With each sad but true fact, Annie edged her way further back behind her new friend. Meggy had to end the painful conversation. Meeting one set of mother's eyes after another, she said, "Let's just think about today, for now. When I left Drumaderry it was gettin' too cold for the children to be dancin' all day in a stone-cold hut. So I'm wonderin' if one of ye might consider allowin' me to teach the lessons in your home, just for today?"

Meggy's heart swelled with admiration at the courage of the women. For even though they knew the terrible risks they were taking, each and everyone had their hand up. Their children cheered with joy. "Now how will I choose without hurtin' anyone's feelin's?" thought Meggy. She came up with a fair plan, which also decreased the risk of the enemy finding out where she was teaching. "For today and tomorrow we'll have our class in the cottage closest to the well. Then for the next two days we'll be dancin' in the cottage farthest from the well. If that works out, we'll go on takin' turns until me time here is up."

The women murmured their agreement. They had just met Dance Mistress Meggy, yet already they knew she was kind, fair and intelligent. Stepping forward, two small blond brothers said, "I'm Pete Dillon." "I'm Pat Dillon." "Our cottage is right there, so you'll be comin' with us today, Miss Meggy." Each taking a hand they led her to their home. The others followed and Annie moved as Meggy's shadow.

The first thing Mrs. Dillon and her boys did was make room for the dancin'. They made quick work of folding up their settle bed, moving the table and setting the benches on top. The boys' grandfather sat on a stool beating out the rhythm on his boudrain. Mistress Meggy's class of ten young dancers filled the cottage to the brim. Wanting to impress Meggy, the biggest lad volunteered to be the lookout. He pretended to repair the thatch on the Dillons' roof while keeping a watch for soldiers.

The morning went by in a flurry of dancing feet, and before the children knew it, their mothers were back. Meggy stayed to help put the Dillon household back in order. As they lifted down the benches, the boys asked, "May Miss Meggy stay for dinner, Mam?"

Even though she was hungry and had no idea when she would eat again, Meggy was embarrassed. So she replied, "Oh, no, that's quite all right. I need to get Annie back before her parents start worryin'."

Mrs. Marjorie Dillon was sure of two things. First, that Annie's parents never worried about her. Second, that there would be not a speck of food for the girls, let alone a caring adult to prepare it. So she said, "If ye stay, Annie can play with me sons after dinner while you and I make a schedule of the homes you will be teachin' in." One look at Annie's hopeful face and Meggy knew what her answer would be.

Spending useful time with Mrs. Dillon was like an antidote to her awful experience with Paddy and Gracie. As nightfall approached, Meggy shuddered to think of returning to their cottage. "I would never trust those two enough to fall asleep there. If they found out about me coins I'd never see them again. And if I lose them now, I won't have time to earn enough again by Christmas. Me family will be homeless."

Looking at Annie, her hair brushed tidy by Mrs. Dillon, she thought, "But if I don't stay, Annie won't get any dance lessons. I need to make a plan that will work for both Annie and me." So Meggy said their thank yous, and, holding the little girl's hand, headed back to her dark and loveless home.

Inside it was as if Paddy and Gracie had not budged since morning. The fire was still out, dirty dishes on the table and the stench of their bodies still filled the air. Meggy was tempted to just take Annie and leave. But the creaking of the door woke the greedy Paddy, "Welcome home me pretties. What did ye bring me to eat?"

Meggy was about to retort that they had nothing and had eaten only at the kindness of strangers, when Annie pulled two fistfuls of boiled pigs' feet out of her pockets. Curiosity made Gracie drag herself up from the covers. She saw her daughter standing there so proudly, her little hands full of food she had stolen for them. She cackled, "That's me Annie. You know how to take care of your mam, don't ye." Then she and Paddy both lunged for the trotters, wrestling them in a dirty tangle on the floor.

Paddy ended up with four, Gracie with two and Annie with none. As they sucked noisily on the juicy bones, Meggy couldn't believe her eyes. She did not know what shocked her more— that Annie had stolen food from the Dillons, or that Paddy and Gracie would take it all, leaving the little girl with nothing.

Shaking her head she said, "It's been a long day. Where am I to sleep?"

Gesturing grandly with a pig's foot, Patty said sarcastically, "Well, Dance Mistress, you may choose any of the fine beds in the fine rooms you see here." Of course there were no other beds, let alone rooms. Even the once best chair was useless. Too lazy to go out for peat, Paddy had broken off the legs for firewood.

Noticing the disapproval on Meggy's face, Gracie said, "What's the matter, Mistress Meggy, too good to sleep in a settle with the rest of us?"

Gracie had no idea how much Meggy wished for their settle at home, "If only I could be tucked up with Da, Mam, and Dan, smellin' the warm sweetness of the peat fire." Leaving her lovely thoughts, she realized with all that she ever knew about wrong, that she should not spend even five minutes in that bed with Gracie and Paddy.

Gracie had her own suggestion, "Well you know Paddy, we do have another spot where Miss Meggy could rest her pretty head!"

Paddy winked back, "Would Maybelle mind sharin' her fine lodgin's?"

Annie spoiled their joke. "How could Maybelle mind? Maybelle's a cow!"

Meggy, who thought sleeping with a cow far preferable to sleeping with them, shocked the jokers by gathering up her belongings. "Annie, will you please show me the way to Maybelle's home?"

Head held high, Dance Mistress Meggy left with as much dignity as if she was going to sleep with a queen in a castle.

Asking questions with each step, Annie led the way, "Are ye really goin' to sleep with Maybelle? Are ye goin' to stay out here, all by yourself? Are ye really not afraid?"

When she got an overwhelming whiff of Maybelle's stall, Meggy began to question her own decision. Peering inside she saw a once beautiful black Kerry cow standing in her own dung. One look at the animal's sore and swollen udder had Meggy talking softly to her, "Oh, ye poor thing. You must be in agony from not bein' milked. Those two good-for-nothin's have left you sufferin' all day, while they lay abed." Grabbing a bucket and pulling a stool under the beast, she gently pulled on the teats. "There ye go, love, give me yer milk and Annie will have a warm drink before bed."

Turning to Annie, the older girl said, "Now if Maybelle is goin' to share her milk with us, we need to be payin' her back. How do ye think we could do that?"

Because she was holding her nose, Annie's voice squeaked. "Miss Maybelle does not want to lie down in that mess. She wants a clean floor that doesn't stink!"

Eyeing an old shovel, Meggy began the dirty job of removing the thick sludge from the floor. When she was done, Annie, who had been exploring a bit said, "On the other side of this little wall there is a big pile of clean straw."

The two girls worked as if they had known each other forever. With a rake that was missing two teeth, the elder moved piles of straw. Using her hands and feet, the younger one arranged it smoothly over the floor and built up quite a pile in the corner. When Meggy asked what she was up to, Annie replied with a smile, "That's your sleepin' spot—piled high and dry." Wanting to keep that smile there, Meggy scooped the little girl up and tossed her gently into the pile. A straw fight followed. Maybelle stared at her guests with a puzzled expression in her big eyes.

As they sat picking the pale straw out of each other's dark curls, Meggy said, "It's time for bed. But first, a nice warm drink of milk." Cupping their hands, the girls ended up with as much milk on their faces as in their mouths.

"Now I'll walk you back to the cottage," said Meggy.

Annie asked worriedly, "Won't you be cold, without even a blanket?"

"Don't you worry," answered Meggy, pulling a blanket from her pack, along with some clothes. "I'm goin' to put these boy clothes on over me dress and wear these boots. Of course I'll be wearin' me cap, so me brains don't freeze up," she teased, noticing just in time who was snoozing inside it. Putting her finger to her lips, she shushed Annie and held out the cap, "Look. This is me friend, Woody."

Annie's eyes grew big. Her rose-red lips made a little "ooo" sound as she looked at the tiny mouse, rolled into a warm, sleepy ball, his tail curled round him. Not wanting to disturb his snooze, both girls blew him kisses goodnight.

Offering the small girl her arm, "Mac" walked her home and gave her a kiss on the cheek. Returning to the shed, Meggy checked to make sure neither the conniving Gracie nor the horrid Paddy were spying on her. She set the cap, with the sleeping mouse inside, on a shelf. Then she buried her pack with the precious treasure inside under the straw. Exhausted, she fell asleep.

Meggy awoke feeling achingly cold. Needing more warmth, she dug up her pack and reburied it where she could sleep curled up against the cow's warm back. She was barely settled when she heard a foot shuffling through straw.

Slowly she reached out for the pitchfork she had left within arm's reach, fearing not only soldiers but also Paddy and Gracie. Knowing surprise was her best chance, she lay as still as death. As the steps shuffled closer she coiled tight, prepared to spring up and lunge forward.

Meggy was forever grateful that Annie had whispered her name. She couldn't bear to picture what might have happened if she hadn't. When the little girl scooted around the cow and plopped down beside her, Meggy exhaled a big shuddering breath.

Annie did not see her terror. "Look, look what I've got for you," she squealed, happily dumping her gift into her friend's lap.

With trembling hands, Meggy fingered warm fabric that smelled faintly of lavender. Instantly she pictured a kind face that could only be Mr. McSorley's Aunt Jessie. The little girl was still chattering, this time muffled from within a cloud of soft fabric. When her sweet face popped out the top she said, "There are two, one for me and one for you. They are big!"

Not able to resist the warmth of the garment, Meggy stood up and let the gown wrap her in the spirit of the woman who was to have been her hostess. Annie looked up at her and clapped her approval. "Now we are sisters. Sisters sleep together."

Too tired to argue or walk Annie back to the cottage, Meggy lay down again with her back nestled up to Maybelle's warmer one. Then she snuggled Annie into the curve of her own body. The two, one a miniature of the other, looked like raven-haired dolls with faint circles of pink, painted by the cold, on their porcelain cheeks.

Not even the cockadoodle-dooing of the neighboring rooster woke them. But it disturbed Gracie, who, having drank too much poteen the night before, had to make a wild dash to the privy. The poor excuse for a mother thought she would find her daughter dawdling in the privy, having for once noticed her gone. But when she opened the door, ready to yell at her Annie, nothing met her but the smell.

While sitting there, a conversation about their cow came back to Gracie. That sent her to the cowshed. Gripping Annie's shoulders with her claw-like hands she felt soft fabric and screeched, "Where did you get this, you thievin' little devil?" Getting a sniff of the lavender she answered her own question. "This smells like the old hag. I'm her niece and everything she owned is mine. And I've a paper to prove it. Now take that off and give it back to me!"

When the sleepy child didn't move fast enough, Gracie flew into a fury. Pulling at a sleeve, she yanked so hard that Annie fell down crying and clutching her shoulder.

That was it for Meggy, who had already removed her own gown. Picking up the pitchfork she stood between Annie and her horror of a mother and threatened, "Touch her again and you'll feel the points of this."

"She's my daughter and I'll do what I want with her," retorted the awful woman.

"Not while I'm here," warned Meggy, lunging forward. The tines whistled close enough to Gracie's dirty ears to give her a good scare. Leaving her daughter behind, the cowardly woman turned and ran. Meggy picked up the frightened child. Making sure Annie's shoulder was not seriously injured, she helped her out of the large gown. Fearing what might happen if Gracie returned with Paddy, she told a white lie. "The Dillons need us to come early today to help them get ready."

Annie nodded. She seemed almost numb. The poor child didn't smile once, even though Meggy chatted cheerfully all the way to the village. One look at the little girl told the kind Mrs. Dillon why they were so early. She had them sharing her family's warm breakfast before they could say, "Good mornin'."

Once Annie was settled, Meggy's own fears surfaced. "What am I goin' to do, now? I've made it impossible to go back to Paddy and Gracie's." She didn't know that very question had been discussed at that very table the night before. Mr. Dillon spoke as if in answer to her silent question. "Meggy, I speak for all the parents. We think it would be easier and safer if you spend the night at the cottage you teach at. Then there will be no need for your dangerous walks at dawn and dusk."

"But," Meggy interrupted.

As if expecting her "but" Mr. Dillon said, "Of course Annie may stay too. She'll…"

Meggy tried to speak again. "But…"

"No buts. I'll be seein' Paddy and Gracie to confirm the plans." Mr. Dillon's firm way reminded her of her da. She knew there was no point arguing. The plans were made and this time she was grateful. Turning to Annie she said, "Is that all right with you?"

Seated between the two boys, the little girl nodded with the beginning of a smile.

And so began the most peaceful three weeks of Meggy's travels as dance mistress.

Like the small homes she held her classes in, her heart was filled with the joy of children dancing. Having Annie with her made Meggy feel like a big sister again, just when she was missing Dan the most. Because the villagers gave Paddy and Gracie a regular sum "from the dance mistress," neither hide nor hair was seen of them. And moving from one cottage to another seemed to keep any secret watcher from noticing anything illegal going on.

Each Friday, Meggy's coin pouch grew fatter. Most evenings, village folks who needed her to write for them arrived. Each small fee brought her closer to the amount she needed. Meggy counted and recounted the coins as December's days passed. "Will I earn enough, soon enough? There will be time to travel to only one more village before Christmas and it will be only for a day or two. What if they don't pay me enough or if I have to leave too soon?" Fortunately Mistress MacGillycuddy was so busy during the day and so tired at night she had little time to worry.

On Meggy's last night in town, the Dillons arranged a farewell dinner. All of the families came. She and Annie had planned a surprise dance for their guests, but neither of them could have guessed the surprise that awaited them. At the end of the meal Mr. Dillon stood and said, "I've an announcement to make. Me wife has always wanted a little girl and me sons a little sister. So we are invitin' young Annie to stay on with us." Turning to her he said, "Paddy and Gracie gave their permission, but the final say is up to you. Would you like to live here with us?"

All eyes turned to the little girl. Annie just stared at Mr. Dillon, as if she couldn't believe her ears. When she looked at Meggy for assurance, the older girl beamed back a message that could only be *yes*. She had been so worried about leaving her little friend behind.

Annie didn't say anything. She just got up quietly and walked to where the lady of the house was sitting. When she held her thin little arms out, Mrs. Dillon picked her up and held her close. Everyone clapped and clapped. Some even wiped a tear or two.

The only reason Annie got down from those loving arms, was to join Meggy in a dance. Insisting that all host couples form a circle, the two girls danced a jig of love and joy around them. Then linking arms with each couple they swung round and round in foursomes of friendship. Finally they curtsied to each couple and asked them to choose a new pair until all were dancing.

Meggy knew her time in Hag's Hollow had ended. She quietly left the room to gather her belongings, leave a thank-you note for the Dillons and change into her boy's clothes. Watching from the doorway, she caught Annie's eye and motioned to her. Not wanting a sad goodbye, Meggy said, "Close your eyes and open your hands."

Annie did just that. When she felt tiny feet and a little whiskered nose sniffing her hands she squealed, "It's Woody! It's Woody! Are you really givin' me Woody?"

"Yes," Meggy answered, "I'm givin' me littlest friend to me sweetest friend." And after kissing them both on the nose, she disappeared into the dark.

Before she got to the well, she saw the shadowy shapes of a man and a donkey. "Oh please, let it be Mr. McSorley and Bessie-Mae." In answer, she heard a voice say, "Well, if it isn't Meggy-Mac MacGillycuddy." Meggy would never have believed she could be so happy to hear Roddy's voice. She was so relieved not to have to make her journey alone that she ran the rest of the way toward him.

"Meggy love, me heart throbs to see you runnin' to meet me," teased Roddy.

She replied quickly, "Oh Roddy, you're still full of yourself, aren't ye? It's Bessie-Mae I'm glad to see." And she threw her arms around the donkey's neck.

11

❖

CHE DUNG MAN

Meggy was hungry for news from home. She hurled questions at Roddy faster than he could answer. "How is Mam? Is she exhausted from doin' all the work alone? What about Dan? Is he still earnin' coins playin' his whistle? And Fiona, is she missin' me?"

"Slow down, Meggy. I can be answerin' only one question at a time," protested Roddy. He was surprised she had not asked even one question about the person he was sure she would ask about first. "I'll be answerin' your questions. But mount up now or we won't reach Glenmullin before dawn," said Roddy, trying to lift her onto Bessie-Mae's back.

Wanting to rob him of the opportunity and hoping to avoid the unceremonious landing of her first mount, Meggy said, "Squat down Roddy, so I can use you as a step up."

He did so reluctantly. While she stood on his back he vowed silently, "You won this round, Miss Meggy MacGillycuddy. But you'll be kissed by me before the night is over."

Trying to settle herself comfortably in front of a pair of bulky but empty creel baskets, Meggy wondered if she really should be riding the donkey. "Roddy, do you think it's too much for Bessie-Mae to be carryin' the creels and me too?"

"Bessie-Mae is used to carryin' both creels, packed full of our deliveries. Just one full basket would weigh more than ye," explained Roddy. "Did you notice the thick blanket I folded over her back for ye?" If Roddy had just stopped there, he would have been all right. But in his desire to win Meggy's praise, he blundered on. "I couldn't help but notice that Bessie's bony back was hard on your...um, your...um, your...," He searched desperately for a way to finish his sentence without offending Meggy.

"Her bony back was hard on my...what, Roddy?" she asked, enjoying his discomfort.

By the time he backtracked and came up with, "was hard on...you," he was grateful the dark hid his blushing. Meggy was laughing so hard she almost fell off the donkey.

Wanting to leave his embarrassment behind, Roddy began answering her questions about her family. "Dan is growin' like a weed. He gives every coin he earns to your mother. Me mam and Fiona's take turns givin' yours a break.

It does her good to walk by the lake or visit with the other women at the well. You know Fiona, she never complains. But I know she is missin' ye. Between us, we make sure Dan has some fun. She takes him for woods walks, huntin' acorns for his collection. When I'm not travelin', he and I romp and wrestle every day after work. Then, together we bring in the peat."

Roddy was such a good friend to her family Meggy felt ashamed for being so hard on him. An awkward silence followed, filled only by the clip clop of Bessie-Mae's hooves.

Roddy broke it. "Would you like to be hearin' about your da?"

Meggy shuddered. "Yes, Roddy. But I'm afraid. Afraid to ask, afraid to hear."

He sighed and looked up at her. "Ah, Meggy, don't you know that if he'd taken a turn for the worse I would have come for ye?"

Her eyes bright with tears, she asked, "Please, tell me now."

They were so involved with their conversation that the usually cautious pair let their guard down. Almost too late, they heard the thundering of horses' hooves. Before she could object or the enemy could round the bend, Meggy felt herself yanked off the donkey's back and stuffed roughly into one of the baskets.

When Roddy shoved her fallen cap on her head and began spreading something horrid on it, she squawked in protest. "Stop it, Roddy! Stop it!" She poked her head up, trying to wipe the disgusting stuff off her cap.

Grabbing her hands, Roddy spoke fiercely, "No, you stop it, Meggy! I'm tryin' to save your life. If anythin' will keep the soldiers from searchin this basket, it will be Bessie-Mae's plops. For once in your life shut up and be still."

The harsh way he spoke to her shocked Meggy to silence. When she heard the too-close shouts of soldiers, her heart began beating as fast as the horses' pounding hooves. When Roddy whispered calming words to her and the donkey, "Be still, Bessie-Mae. Be still, Meggy." She did as she was told.

Then, as she listened, Roddy put on the performance of his life.

He began wandering about the road picking up horse and donkey dung left by previous four-legged travelers. When a loud command stopped the troop right beside the donkey and her hiding passenger, Roddy began to fill the other creel basket with dung.

"Who goes there?" shouted the sergeant.

Roddy hoped the rank smell would discourage the soldiers from investigating his load thoroughly. "Sir, it's just me, the Dung Man, collectin' me nightly load."

Holding his neck cloth to his nose, the sergeant turned to his men and said in disbelief, "I knew the Irish were a stupid people, but this beats all."

Turning back to the Dung Man he asked, "What is your name and why are you collecting dung?"

If she hadn't been so scared, Roddy's lie would have set Meggy to giggling. He answered, "Me name is Seamus Fox.

I collect the dung because me father did, as me grandfather did, as me great-grandfather…"

Wanting to stop the dullard from droning on forever, the sergeant ordered, "Stop your blabbering." Turning to his troop, he raised his eyebrows and said sarcastically, "Perhaps if I speak louder and slower he'll understand me question." Looking right into the Dung Man's face he asked, "WHAT—DO—YOU—USE—THE—DUNG—FOR?"

"Oh, it's most useful, sir." Holding up a sample, Roddy continued, "When it's fresh we use it to patch our roofs. When it's dry it makes a fine fire. And me good wife has come up with a recipe for a delicious dung bun," beamed "Seamus the Dung Man" proudly.

Meggy could hear one of the soldiers gagging. Just then the sergeant's horse lifted his fine black tail and deposited a steaming fresh plop on the road. With a look of simple gratitude, the Dung Man said, "Why thank ye, sir. Me wife's batter will be all the better from addin' this fresh servin' from your fine horse."

Not able to stand the stupid man or the stench any longer, the sergeant made ready to lead his troop on. He rallied his men to the task, "We're searching for a treasonous dance mistress named Meggy. She's been teaching the heathen dancing. We've followed her from village to village, just missing her. But not tonight. A reputable informer told us that she just left Hag's Hollow and is on her way to Glenmullin, down this very road. We've got troops out all over it. She'll not escape us!"

Meggy was spared witnessing what happened next.

Pointing his bayonet at Roddy's throat, the leader demanded, "Have you seen her?"

Gulping, Roddy answered, "No sir, I've seen nothin' but me donkey and me dung."

Drawing a sharp line of blood across Roddy's neck, the sergeant warned, "If I find out you've helped her, I'll be back to slit you open and stuff you with your precious dung."

Whipping his horse to a start, he led his troop thundering off down the road. But his threat remained in the blood dripping down the Dung Man's neck.

Sensing Meggy's movements, Roddy said, "Don't be showin' yourself until I tell ye. Just one soldier takin' just one last look back could reveal your presence. One shot from their guns would…" Such horror filled his mind that Roddy could not finish his sentence.

Unable to resist taking a look at her enemy, Meggy raised her eyes just above the basket. The bloody line staining the front of Roddy's neck like some horrid scarlet neck cloth froze her with its fearful reality. Roddy shoved her back down, hissing, "STAY DOWN SO I DON'T GET CAUGHT TRANSPORTIN' A TREASON-COMMITTIN' DANCE MISTRESS!"

Never before had Roddy spoken so harshly or honestly to her. His words, like sharp fingers of fear, wrapped themselves tightly round her heart. From the stinking confines of the basket she whispered one more question, "What are we goin' to do, Roddy?"

He answered, "I'll be stickin' to our original route, unless another troop comes upon us. If it does, we'll have to be leavin' the road to hide."

Each hour, each mile passed agonizingly slowly. Meggy's back and knees were cramping from being stuffed too tight for too long in the basket. The plops were sliding down her cap and into her hair. From there, the disgusting stuff slid down onto her face. When she felt like she couldn't stand one more minute of the dark and the dung she began to repeat over and over, "Better dirty than dead. Better dirty than dead. Better dirty than dead."

"Listen, Meggy," said Roddy. All she could here was the burbling of a stream. Roddy led Bessie-Mae off the road. As the donkey picked her way over rough ground, down into a hiding glen, Meggy was bumped and bruised by the jostling basket. Stopping again to listen, only an owl questioned their presence.

Meggy was only too glad, this time, to feel Roddy's arms lifting her up and out, even though she was embarrassed by the stench of herself. Her legs were useless. She had to hold onto Bessie-Mae until they would hold her up again. The minute she could walk, Meggy headed straight for the stream. Its December cold made her fingers ache, but she plunged her hands in and kept them there till she scrubbed every last bit of dung off. Picking some spongy moss from the bank, she wiped and washed the disgusting stuff off her hair, her face and then her clothes. Finally the stench was diminished enough for her to notice the fresh clean smell of watermint. Picking some of its leaves she crushed them and rubbed their minty fragrance on her hair.

Refreshed, she turned to Roddy, who having washed only his hands, was sitting beneath an old oak, looking tired and pale. "Will you let me tend your wound?" He nodded *yes.* Meggy knew from watching her mam that she must get all the dirt out. Using fresh bits of moss, she gently worked away till the wound was a clean red line across his throat.

Suddenly overcome by the risk her friend had taken for her, she sat back and took his hand. "Roddy, you saved me life and nearly lost your own doin' it! I can't bear to think what would have happened if that soldier had slashed your neck one bit deeper."

This time he did not have to steal a kiss. Overwhelmed with gratitude, Meggy leaned over and kissed him gently on the lips. It was the sweetest and briefest of kisses, like no more than the flutter of a butterfly's wings. But Roddy would remember it forever. He sat in shocked and silent pleasure while she searched her pack. Taking out her apron, she tore two long strips from the bottom, tied them together and wrapped them round his neck.

Smiling at him she said, "That's as fancy a bandage as you'll ever have. It's trimmed with the first bits of lace me clumsy hands ever made. Is it too tight?"

Roddy wanted to say, "No part of you could be clumsy, Meggy." But all he managed was, "Just fine, thank ye." Getting to his feet he went to Bessie-Mae who was enjoying a chew of watermint. "Now, old girl, it's your turn for a bit of a clean-up."

Releasing the slip bottom, they dumped the dung out of one basket and rinsed its stinking cargo off in the stream. Having used their blankets to dry themselves and Bessie, they could not dry the inside. "One hour of sunshine would do it, but that we don't have. So we'll have to go on as is," said Roddy, holding out his arms to help Meggy back in.

"Roddy, I can't bear to get back in, especially since I'm so cold and the creel is so wet. Couldn't I be walkin' along with ye, for a bit?" she asked with her irresistible smile.

"All right, Meggy. But be sure your hair is covered by your cap. You must look more like young Mac and less like the beautiful Dance Mistress Meggy," answered Roddy, trying to tuck a few stray curls up under her still damp cap.

Then the two young "lads," one tall and broad-shouldered, one shorter and slighter, led the donkey back to the roadside. From behind a trio of alders, they watched for any sign of danger and listened for hoofbeats. Hearing only the mellow night notes of the thrush, they stepped back onto the road. The moon shone bright to light their way.

One danger they had not considered was a roadblock, especially not round the first bend. The image of blood running down Roddy's neck was too fresh in Meggy's mind. She knew she could not let him risk his life for her again. Hoping none of the soldiers ahead had noticed the two "lads" yet, she grabbed her pack and ducked behind a blackthorn hedge.

She whispered, "Roddy, go on to the roadblock alone. If it isn't the same troop, I'll be able to escape well into the woods while they waste time tauntin' the Dung Man."

When a soldier shouted, "Stop in the name of the Penal Code," Roddy was given no choice. Wanting to give Meggy as much time as possible, he dawdled toward them. He had not taken three steps when he was surprised to hear her whisper again, "Roddy, tear off the bandage or the lace may tell them you've not been travelin' alone."

Taking his time, he bent down again and again to gather up his treasures. The very first plop went into the too-clean pannier wrapped round a lace-trimmed cloth.

As Meggy ran into the woods, she heard the soldiers yelling, "Hurry up! Don't keep the king's own soldiers waiting." She ran and ran and ran until the only sound she heard was the pounding of her own heart.

Her feet led her into a waterlogged place, where bats flew low enough to skim her cap. Closing her eyes to say a quick prayer for Roddy, she stumbled forward. Meggy knew from the quaking mat of decaying plants tangled round her boots that she must tread carefully. She had stumbled into a bog.

Stretching one booted foot back at a time, she felt for drier ground. She reached up to take hold of two dangling willow branches, trying to steady herself in the dark ooze. "I can't return to the road. But if I continue runnin' into the dark of the bog, I may step in over me head and disappear forever. What am I to do?"

* * *

Roddy was having trouble stalling the soldiers. If they had been a group new to the Dung Man, he could probably have delayed them longer with his antics. But they were half of the earlier troop. They had a good but short laugh at his expense and then tried to send him on. "Hey ho, Your Royal Stench. Now we've had the distinct displeasure of meeting you not once, but twice, Sir Dung. So pass through quickly before your stink sticks to us."

By turning their horses sideways, two of the soldiers opened a way through the roadblock. When Roddy did not budge, they crowded their mounts so close that the small clouds of warm air from their horses' nostrils blended with those from Bessie-Mae.

"Get out of the way, Dung Man," yelled one.

Roddy may have been outnumbered but he wasn't out-smarted. "But, excuse me, Sir Soldiers, I can't be movin' yet."

"Dung Man, move, or I'll widen that slit in your neck," warned one, brandishing his bayonet-tipped musket.

"But, Sir Soldier, it was your sergeant who told me to stay here," said Roddy.

"What do you mean, our sergeant told you to stay here?" yelled the another soldier.

"Sir Soldier Number Two, he said to wait and give you a message," Roddy explained.

"What message, you idiot?" yelled Number One.

"Spit it out!" hollered Number Two.

Roddy said, "Sir Sergeant and his soldiers went after that girl with black curls!"

The one soldier asked the other, "Shall I kill him or does he really have a message?"

Number Two Soldier asked, "Do you mean the raven-haired dance mistress?"

Out of delays, Roddy pointed to the opposite side of the road from where Meggy had escaped and said, "She went that way. Your sergeant and the others went that way too."

Soldier Number One boasted, " I'll be the one to capture that law-breaking beauty."

"No, you won't!" argued Number Two. "The dance mistress will be mine!"

Whipping their horses into a fury, they charged off, with the others galloping behind.

The last soldier, older and slower but perhaps wiser, grabbed Roddy by the neck and threatened, "Dung Man, if you've lied to us, we'll be back for you." Then he knocked Roddy out with the butt of his musket and kicked him viciously in the ribs. Snarling, "That will make sure you're still here," he rode off to join the others.

For Roddy, who would not wake from the blow until morning, the night was over. But not for Meggy.

12

❖

The Bog Beauties

Meggy had just decided to take shelter in the massive willow for the night when, despite Roddy's best efforts, the sounds of angry soldiers came at her from every corner of the woods. They cursed as their horses crashed through thickets. The thorns clawed viciously at man and beast alike. Surrendering to nature, a few riders dismounted, tying their mounts to a stand of yews before setting out on foot.

Others charged on and were dealt with severely by the woods. Meggy heard their sounds and guessed their meaning. One soldier, galloping down a dark sheep path, was suddenly dismounted by a low-hanging branch. The conking sound of the skull of a careless rider meeting hardwood at high speed was unmistakable.

When Meggy heard a whooshing sound, she pictured a mainly road-ridden horse's hoof stepping into a hare hole. The horse had pitched forward, ejecting the rider. She guessed, "I'll hear a man cursing next." She was rewarded with a loud "*%#*!!!" "There it is, he's landed in a thorny bush,"she told herself with satisfaction.

But Meggy knew better than to get too confident. "I can only be sure that two soldiers are down but I don't know for how long. I don't know how many others are still lookin' for me or how close they are." Without time to disentangle herself from the bog or take refuge in the willow, the soldiers' presence forced her to remain as still as a standing stone. Held up only by her aching arms and the willow branches, she could feel more than see her hunters. She peered into the slices the moonlight cut through the boggy woods. More spots were dark than light, so Meggy had to depend on her ears to warn her of approaching enemies.

It wasn't long before a cautious rider slowly clip-clopped his horse toward her. While she tried to become one with the dark, he dismounted right under the willow, to stretch and look up at the full moon framed by the lacy willow leaves. As the soldier lingered, Meggy felt every part of her body try to break out of the freeze she had willed them into. Her left leg tried to tremble. Her nose itched for a sneeze. Finally, looking for a drink for his mount, he stepped forward. Meggy was never sure whether it was the eerie night touches of the willow tips or a burst of bats, but suddenly the horse reared up.

Trying to stay out of range of flailing hooves while trying to catch hold of the reins, the rider took one too many steps backward. Before he knew it, he was stuck in the boggy quagmire right up to his waist. Only the grasp he had finally found on the reins kept him standing. Suddenly, as if sensing her rider's need, the frightened steed settled. The horse's steady pull on the reins kept him from losing his balance and falling into the bog. But even with her help, he could not pull himself out.

Looking across at the helpless man, Meggy started to feel sorry for him. Especially when he started calling, "Help! Help! Help me! Somebody help me!"

Meggy was just considering reaching out for him when she heard the curses of men unused to running in the woods. "Where are you?" they called.

"Here! Here!" answered the man, his voice and his arms growing weaker.

Despite the bobbing light of their lantern, the night woods hid the men's friend—the dance mistress—from them. They seemed to circle the area forever. The trapped soldier grew weaker. Leaning forward, Meggy tried to see if the man or the bog was winning. A slice of moonlight pointed to a small dark circle on the ground between her and the horse. The night wind ruffling her hair told her what it was. "Me cap! It's fallen off! The soldiers' lantern will identify its Irishness and evidence of me presence. What can I do? What can I do?"

Meggy panicked, then a memory of the owner of the cap cleared her mind. "I can't let Da and me family down. If I don't escape, all me work—all the risks Roddy and the families took—will be worth nothin'. I must not be captured now. I will not be captured now!"

Too soon for Meggy and almost too late for their bog-bound friend, the soldiers arrived. As they tried to reach him, she tried to think above the pounding of her heart. "While they are tryin' to save him, they may not notice me cap. But afterward they will. Once it is discovered, I will be trapped in the light of their lantern. I can't take that risk." She was for once grateful that her clothing was dull and dark.

Checking the rescue, she saw that in their efforts to save the first soldier, two others had fallen in. Making sure her pack was securely on, Meggy started to let her hands slide down the willow branches and herself slip bit by bit, into the bog. Shuddering, she let its disgusting sliminess clothe her in a suit of sludge. Hanging onto one willow branch after another, Meggy silently pulled herself closer to her cap and to her enemy. Finally she was so close she could see the sinews stretched tight on the horse's neck. She shuddered, "I can smell me enemies' sweat. I must do it now, before they see me." Within arm's reach of where the bog met solid ground, Meggy was almost flat out, immersed up to her nose like some long ago reptilian creature. "Now I just have to reach out and pull me cap out of sight. But when is the right time?" Meg shivered as the cold oozed down her neck.

Slapping a slithery wetness from his face a soldier shouted, "I hate this heathen country."

"Well, I'll not be beaten by one of its disgusting bogs," said another. "Help me get a rope to Toby. Then we'll wind the other end round that willow."

Meggy knew the moment had come. Taking one last look to make sure no eyes were on her, she moved with the stealth of a pickpocket. One second, her cap was there. The next, it was gone.

Her chance of being discovered increased with every moment she remained in the bog. She was closer than ever to her enemy, close enough to see their angry eyes. All she wanted was to climb out of the disgusting damp and decay. The soldiers made that impossible. To reach her cap, she'd had to let go of one branch. Now she was too low to grab another and drag herself back through the bog, away from her enemy.

"What am I goin' to do?" thought Meggy desperately. "I can't go forward onto land. I can't go backward deeper into the bog. Me left arm is all that is keepin' me nose up out of the sludge. Me shoulder feels like it's bein' stretched to the breakin' point. Am I goin' to die here—without me family? Just be swallowed up by the bog—never to be seen again? Are me hard-earned coins goin' down with me—leaving me family homeless?"

The harsh curses of the soldiers snapped her out of her dark thoughts. All but the original soldier were out of the bog. Four big brutes now stood between the horse and the willow, close enough that Meggy could have reached out and touched their boots. "I can't stay here. One swing of their lantern, one slip of a boot and I'll be found."

She had foretold her own future. Right then a lantern's beam fell across her face. "Someone's there. Someone's there!" yelled the soldier. "I saw a face, a white face—peering up at me out of the ooze," he shouted, pointing to where Meggy had just been.

The other four saw nothing. "Toby, you've been too long in the bog," joked one.

"And too long at the bottle," laughed another.

"I saw a woman's face, stark white with dark eyes," insisted Toby.

"Well then, where is she now?" asked the third.

"She must have dunked under," Toby insisted.

"Well then, she must be a mermaid, because no human could stay under that long," said one. The others taunted Toby, "Was she beautiful, Toby? Come on, Toby. Share your Bog Beauty with us."

Indeed, desperate Meggy had ducked under the surface of the bog, and had found tree roots to hold on to. When at last, gasping, she had pulled herself forward and up and suddenly felt night air on her head, she was certain a soldier would grab her hair and yank her out. But nothing happened. She opened her eyes, and discovered her head and arms were in a small root-tangled hollow, just above the ooze of the bog and just below the ground. She realized, "I've seen little caves like this when the level of the bog drops."

Her investigation of the hollow was disturbed by the taunting voice of one of the men above. "How about we catch us a mermaid?" The others quickly joined in as he started jabbing the dark bog with a long sharp branch. Almost immediately it tore its jagged way down Meggy's leg. She curled her body around, trying to fit all of her into the too-small hollow. The bony roots prodding her back made her feel like she was sharing her hideaway with a bent and broken skeleton. The blood worms, whose sleep she had disturbed, were now crawling over her neck and into her ears. Only the evil of the men above kept her from screaming.

Then bits of dirt and sticks began to fall down on her. The weight of the four bullies, jostling for the best mermaid-spearing position, was threatening to collapse her shelter. In their rowdiness, two of the big soldiers knocked each other down. Their dual landing caused a heavy root to dislodge and fall on Meggy's head. It nearly knocked her out.

"I must make the soldiers move or I'll be left with nothing but to die in the bog or at the hands of me enemies." The sting of the cut on her leg gave her an idea for a game of her own. The root in her right hand was loose—indeed, she was surprised to discover it felt like it was wrapped in something. But there was no time to investigate. She grasped the loose root with her right hand and held tight to the strongest still-attached root with her left. Ducking under the sludge, Meggy stretched herself close enough to the still bogged-down Toby to let the length of the root in her right hand brush across his thigh. Then she retreated quickly to her hideaway.

Toby's terrified shriek pierced through the rowdy banter of the others. "She touched me! She slithered past my leg! She touched me! Get me out of here!"

His anguished face showed the others the truth of his terror more than a hundred words could have done. As they watched in horror, his whole left side jerked suddenly downwards, as if grabbed by some hungry sea creature. Only the fingers frozen around his horse's reins kept him from going under. The other soldiers stood still, frozen too, in a tableau of fear.

Meggy's haven stopped collapsing. Abover her, the soldiers were utterly silent. "Why would they be so suddenly quiet?" Then she heard a distinctly female voice—heard it sobbing. The men above heard it too, a crying voice, floating up from the depths of the bog. They thought it was calling, "To—beeeee; To—beeee; To—beeee."

The next sound was the terrified whinny of his horse. Again it reared up on its back legs. Its powerful front hooves were striking the air, as if trying to destroy the haunting cries that set it frothing at the mouth. When the spooked horse landed, it took off so fast that Toby popped out of the sludge like pus from a boil. No more able to uncramp his hands from the reins than his horse was able to stop running, he was dragged from the bog on his belly.

As the sounds became a chorus of eerily sad songs and haunting sighs, the other soldiers could not mount their horses fast enough. They rode off, unaware they had left not only the traitorous dance mistress but also a treasure to the sighing beauties of the bog.

Still grasping the root in her right hand, Meggy cautiously emerged from her safe haven to wade out of the bog. Unafraid, she turned to seek the singers whose eerie songs had freed her. Off in the curve of a cove she saw them, first appearing as small boats lit pearly white by the moon. Then they floated toward her, against the black velvet night. As she knew they would, the boats soon began to look more like the swans they were, their graceful necks now visible. Closer still, and the moonlight gave them dark eyes and leaf-gold bills. They arrived at Meggy's feet without making a ripple on the dark of the bog. "Thank you, me lovelies. The timing of your arrival is almost enough to make me believe in fairy tales again."

Stopping only long enough to look into her eyes, they floated on. "Since I've no better guide, I'll follow you." With the root in her right hand to steady her, their pearl-glow led Meggy's feet along the bank without one tumble in the darkness. Where a pair of silvery birches guarded a stream's flow into the bog, the swans entered. They led Meggy deep into a hollow and around a bend. Where a scatter of stones stepped across the fresh water, they stopped to bathe.

Fears almost forgotten, she watched in delight. The swans dipped their long necks down until their heads disappeared under water and their feather-curled bottoms tipped up to the stars. Surfacing, they sparkled like diamonds as the moon lit the droplets of water beading up on their feathers. The cleaner they became, the dirtier Meggy felt. The bog had oozed over every inch of her. Dirt had dug itself in between her fingers and toes. Her ears were unbearable twin cesspools of slime and bloodworms.

"Those cowards won't be returnin' tonight, will they?" Meggy asked aloud. "I can't stand meself one minute longer." Stepping onto the first rock she dipped her fingers. Immediately she dropped her belongings, shucked her shoes and plunged in, stinking feet first. "Jesus, Mary and Joseph! It's goin' to be an icy bath!"

By the time Meggy reached the big, middle rock, only the moonlight clothed her. She was so cold her teeth chattered, yet she did not stop washing until she had scrubbed every bit of herself, her dress carrying the coins, and the rest of her belongings. All except for one.

She laid her clothes on rocks or over branches to await the first drying light of day. The bite of the December night on her bare skin made her realize the folly of washing every bit of her clothing. "Good job, Meggy. You've just made sure that your body will be found not only clean but frozen stiff and stark naked too!"

Looking around for something warm, she noticed the swans were sleeping nestled down into their own pillow-soft bodies. Their heads were tucked cozily under their wings.

They had chosen to sleep at the foot of one of the birch trees. Tiptoeing closer, Meggy saw that the small hollow the trees were rooted in was covered with a thick pad of cushion moss. The swans must have slept there often because the moss was dotted with downy soft feathers. Mixed in with the white of the feathers were the birches' fallen leaves. Meggy sat down between the swans and the tree. Curling up on her side, she covered herself with dry leaves.

Perhaps she dreamt their songs, sweet only to the Irish. But the cold and lonely Meggy knew it was the swans' lullaby that lulled her into a sleep as peaceful as their beauty.

13

❖

Lost and Alone

Dreaming he was dancing with a dark-haired fairy, Roddy woke to a kiss. When the sloppy face made him realize Bessie-Mae, not a fairy, was kissing him, he sat straight up. A wave of dizziness knocked him back down. Sitting up again cautiously, he saw two Bessies peering down at him. When he shook his head to clear his vision, pain jabbed his right temple. The throbbing lump made him remember his attacker and his promise to return. Roddy knew he had to get away fast. Hearing the burble of a stream, he crawled to it and splashed cold water on his face. Then, despite the flames of pain tearing up his side, he dragged himself up a massive oak until he was on his feet again.

Looking around, he felt confused. "This looks like the

glen where Meggy washed the dung off. But that can't be. The soldier hit me at the roadblock, which is well out of the woods, up around the bend in the road."

His legs buckling, Roddy sank to the ground and leaned back against the solid oak. The minute he closed his eyes, he could feel Meggy leaning over him and gently leaving her kiss on his lips. "Jesus, Mary and Joseph, I've dreamt of Meggy kissin' me a thousand times. But somehow, I know that kiss was real. That it happened right here under this tree. But how did I get back here?"

The memory of the kiss was followed too closely by the vision of Meggy running off into the woods alone. "Did me lie send the soldiers off on a wild goose chase? Or did they suspect me tall tale and double back? Where is the rest of that troop of bullies?" worried Roddy. Dropping his aching head into his hands, his mind was tortured with visions of musket-armed soldiers, circling closer and closer to his Meggy.

Calling Bessie to him, he used all his strength to tip the baskets from her back. But when he tried to mount her, the excruciating pain in his side kept him from pulling himself up. Determined to ride Bessie to Meggy's rescue, he walked her to a rock and mounted. Too dizzy to sit up, he wrapped his arms around her neck and laid his head on hers. Escape from the pain and nightmare fears came to Roddy at last, with the deep sleep of unconsciousness.

* * *

It was not the soft sad song of the swans that woke Meggy, but rather the "Peeweet, peeweet," of a lapwing soaring overhead. If not for the down-feathered hollow she lay in, she might not have believed her memories of the swans. Alone now and shivering, she jumped up to grab her clothes. "They won't be dry yet, but they'll be better than nothing." But Meggy's fingers discovered dry where she expected damp. Running from bush to rock, she gathered up her clothing, putting some on as she went. Stopping only to inspect her lace tunic, Meggy folded it with a sigh of relief. Where last night it had been dyed a brackish black and embroidered with slugs and sludge, there was now hope it might be white again. Bending over to pull on her boots, she was surprised to discover her shadow to be mid-day short, "No wonder the swans are gone, me clothes are dry and me belly is so empty it is achin'. I've slept past noon."

Warmer and dressed as a boy, Meggy pulled her cap on. Tucking her curls up, she had a sweet memory of Roddy helping her. "Oh Roddy, where are ye now? Did you make it through the roadblock? Did those awful soldiers hurt ye because of me?" she shuddered.

She thought to go back to look for him, but the memory of his harsh and honest words stopped her. Reluctantly Meggy realized that the presence of a "treason-commitin' dance mistress" could do her friend much more harm than good. She spoke aloud, as if hoping the wind would carry her words to him, "Roddy, for now we must travel our paths alone. But I believe, by the strength of our friendship, we will find each other alive, well, and home again in Copperkin."

Thoughts of home brought her reason for traveling rushing back. "The soldiers stopped us before we had barely left Hag's Hollow. Even with Bessie to ride and Roddy to guide me way, I'd have had only two days in Glenmullin, and now I've lost a day and a night. I can't go home without enough money to pay the rent!"

In desperation she untied her dress. The coins glittered so, as they spilled out across the dull ground, that Meggy's heart soared at the sight of them. But as she picked and pushed them into neat piles of five, her heart dropped. No matter how many times she counted and recounted there were fewer coins than when she had left Hag's Hollow. The bog must have taken its due. "No! No! No! I don't have enough. I don't have near enough to keep me family from becomin' homeless."

Feeling cold, tired and hopeless, Meggy cried so hard the front of her shirt became as wet as it had been the night before. A series of little bumps on her leg finally made her look up. A pygmy shrew, smaller than her palm, was trying to climb over her leg. "Poor little blind fella, gettin' over me leg must be as big a climb for you as climbin' the Purple Mountains would be for me," she sniffed.

As he bumped her leg again, she said, "You're not givin' up, are ye? Let me give you a boost. There now, off you go and find a tasty worm to nibble on."

She gave herself a good talking-to. "Get up Meggy! Sittin' here, fillin' the stream with your tears is not goin' to get you fed or home. All may not be lost. I have proven meself as a wage-earner. Perhaps Lord Black will accept this for now and give us time to earn more. I have to try. It's our last chance."

Checking to make sure she was not going to step on the shrew, Meggy saw that the little fellow was stuck again. This time his "mountain" was a sheath of deerskin, her bog find, dropped and forgotten. While giving him a boost, she said, "You are a wee thing aren't you—not even half the size of Woody." Picking up the sheath she gave it a quick rinse. The sludge must have been acting like glue, because the widest end opened to reveal a shiny handle.

Meggy's heart started to beat doubletime and fill with the warmth that is hope. She'd heard tales of bog treasures. Could she possibly be holding one? Gripping the handle in one hand, she slid the sheath off with the other. There, revealed in all its golden glory, was a magnificent sword. The noon sun glinted off its brilliant shine, kept untarnished for untold years by the magic of the bog. "How beautiful—its jewels are as blue as County Kerry's lakes and as green as her valleys!"

Taking the handle in both hands, she held it up to the sun. Gold, sapphire, and emerald shone so brightly they bedazzled her, blocking out any sight of things dark or dangerous. In the dazzling colors, Meggy could picture Boadicea, the warrior queen, holding the sword, her hair falling in red-gold waves past her waist, her tunic rippling with the colors of a sapphire sea and her eyes as fiercely green as the emeralds.

The weight and beauty of the sword made Meggy feel connected to all the brave women in Ireland's past. She stared at the sword, hoping it was real and not just a figment of her exhausted mind and empty belly. As she circled each jewel with the tip of her finger the hairs on the back of her neck stood up, not with fear, but with dawning excitement. "Just one of these jewels might be enough to allow us MacGillycuddys to buy our cottage and never be at Lord Black's mercy again.

"Wait till Dan sees this sword, his eyes will pop right out of his head. And Fiona, she'll be so glad to know we won't have to move. And Roddy—well it would only be fair to be sharin' it with him."

Never having had any money, Meggy's mind reeled with possibilities. "We could be gettin' a doctor for Da. We could be buildin' him and Mam their own bedroom. And books— we could be buyin' books, lots of books for Dan and me. Maybe even more Robin Hood tales."

Thoughts of the immense value of the sword and the responsibility of owning such a treasure sobered Meggy. She sat down to think. "Everyone who sees this sword will want it for their own. Some will do anythin' to make it their own." Remembering the bloody line drawn across Roddy's neck by the soldier, the evil informers in every village, and the greedy eyes of Paddy and Gracie, she shuddered and

reached for the sheath. A glimpse of soldier-red at the edge of the wood had her on her feet and brandishing the sword in an instant. A red grouse burst from the bush.

A big gasp of air got her breathing again. Meggy knew the flash of red could just have easily been a soldier. "I must hide this sword and head quickly home." Sliding the sword into the sheath, she slipped her pants down and bound the sheath to her waist with a band of material from her apron. Shorter strips of cloth secured it knee and thigh. Using a leafy branch, she brushed out her footprints, the only evidence of her night's stay. Some downy feathers made her sigh. "Maybe someday, when Ireland is ours again, I'll return and sleep with the swans once more."

Feeling totally lost, she stood looking in all directions. "Which way do I go? I don't know where to take me first step. At least I have the sun to guide me," thought Meggy. "I know Hag's Hollow is west of Copperkin. That way must be west, because the sun is now edgin' down slightly. This stream runs the opposite way. Maybe if I follow it, I won't end up goin' round in circles. Maybe it will lead me home."

She looked like a slight lad with a bad leg. The heavy sword slowed her down and made it hard to climb over rocks and fallen trees. The woods seemed filled with the possibility of soldiers, hiding behind every tree or waiting around every bend in the creek. She was so afraid they might sneak up on her from behind, her neck was sore from constantly looking back.

Finally hunger pangs stopped her. In her wish to get home as soon as possible she had been ignoring the sounds of her belly for hours. The sludge of the bog had destroyed whatever food had been in her pack, anyway. "Here I am, with a treasure worth enough to buy a feast for everyone in Kerry, and there is not a scrap to buy," she sighed. Just then a noisy jay deposited a mess on the knee of her pants. This set Meggy ranting. "First it was donkey dung, then bog slime and bloodworms. And now you drop your dirty splat on me!"

Grabbing up some dry leaves, she began crossly scraping the reddish mess off, "Red, it's red! Why is your mess red?" Looking around, she discovered her answer and something to eat too. Meggy couldn't pick the berries fast enough. By the time she stopped, her hands and her mouth were a definite cranberry red. Wrapping some more berries in leaves, she tucked them in her pack for later.

Meggy followed the stream's every bend and turn. Scrambling up and over a particularly steep bank she complained, "You just couldn't be a straight and pleasin' little stream, could ye? I would rather grassy banks filled with berry bushes instead of nettles!" Rounding another bend, the stream presented a serious dilemma. "Two branches! Two branches! How am I goin' to be findin' me way home now?" shouted Meggy. Sitting down, she burst into tears. "I've found this sword. It's worth more than enough to pay our rent. But it's all useless, because I'll never find me way home in time to pay it."

Something rustling through the bushes, downstream on the right branch, sent Meggy diving behind a rock for cover. She lay still as stone, hoping that whoever it was would just keep going. When she heard hooves picking their way across the stream, she tried desperately to retrieve the sword from the ties that bound it to her.

The hoof sounds came closer, clip-clopping in her direction. When they could get no closer, they stopped. Unable to retrieve the sword, Meggy pressed herself into the rock. She thought she could feel eyes looking down on her. Terrified the next sound would be the blast of a musket, she heard instead a moan. Then she felt hot breath on her neck. Unable to stay still a moment longer, she looked up.

What she saw was a donkey, a donkey with an obviously wounded man half falling off her back. Two thoughts flashed through Meggy's mind. First, the man was not wearing a red uniform and two, the enemy never rode donkeys. Incredulously she realized, "That's not just any donkey, it's Bessie-Mae. If it's Bessie, the man must be…!"

Meggy was on her feet before she could finish her thought. As she led Bessie-Mae to a grassy mound, the movement set her passenger to moaning again. "Oh Roddy, at least if you're moanin' you're alive." Making sure he was secure, she moved from side to side, trying to determine where his injuries were. A huge lump on his head told her why he was barely conscious. When her gentle probing on the left side of his chest caused him to pull away and moan in pain, she suspected broken ribs.

172

Moving close to his ear she spoke softly, "Roddy, Roddy can ye hear me? It's Meggy. Bessie-Mae brought you right to me."

"Me battered brain must be playin' tricks on me," thought Roddy. Forcing his eyes open, he asked, "Meggy, is it really you?"

Laying her hand on his cheek, she gulped back tears and said, "Yes, Roddy. It is me. I'm goin' to take you home. Then our mams will have you feelin' fine in no time."

Before she even finished her sentence, he drifted off again. She continued talking. "How am I goin' to get you home safely? I should be bindin' your ribs so your every breath doesn't feel like a knife thrust. But I'd need to get you down to do it properly. And if I can't get you back up...?" Meggy couldn't go on. She couldn't bear the thought of leaving Roddy while she went for help. She couldn't bear the possibility of the soldiers finding him and finishing the job they had begun. Most of all she couldn't bear to have someone else she loved die or never be themselves again. Tears streaming down her cheeks, she threw back her head and screamed at the sky, "No! No! Don't take him away! Do you hear me? Don't take away his body or his mind!"

The sun was far to the west now, and noticing it returned Meggy from her rant to what must be done. Since she could not bind Roddy's ribs, she firmly stuffed her other dress full of soft grasses. His shirt tail was already out, so she gently pushed the pillow up and under his sore side to protect it from Bessie's bony back.

Looking at her threadbare blanket, she wished there were two. But keeping him from falling off Bessie was more important than keeping him warm, so Meggy ripped it into strips. By knotting some together, she secured her friend to the donkey as best she could. Turning her back, she reached into her pants and finished removing the sword from her body. Using those strips, she fashioned a set of loops that would hide the sword between Bessie's and Roddy's bodies, while leaving the handle within her reach. Practicing pulling the sword out, she hoped she would not have to use it. But use it she would, if anyone tried to hurt Roddy or steal the treasure.

While tying a cold cloth over Roddy's head wound, Meggy let Bessie drink her fill. The evening sky told her there would be no time for stops if they were to reach home tonight. And tonight it must be—not just for her family's sake, but for Roddy's too.

Since he and Bessie-Mae had come by the right branch, Meggy was hopeful the left branch would lead them home. The night darkened Meggy's spirits, and she wished Roddy was walking where she was, confidently leading the way. It was not an easy journey. Any but the flattest banks sent Roddy sliding off the donkey. It took all Meggy's strength to shove him back up, so often they simply walked through the slippery-bottomed stream.

Meggy's concern for her friend helped her to ignore the blisters on her feet, the thorn scratches on her face and the two-day hunger in her belly. But soon every bend in the stream, every rocky bank, every little glen started to blur. Meggy feared they would never see any sign of home. When they rounded a bend to discover a fallen tree blocking their path, she dropped down onto it, too tired even to be angry.

Through his changing states of consciousness, Roddy must have felt Bessie stop. He surprised Meggy by anxiously calling for her. Jumping to her feet, she stroked his head. "I'm here, Roddy, and I'll not be leavin' ye." His eyes were filled with fear and pain. "You know, don't ye, that you're in the hands—or should I say, hands and hooves—of two most capable females. Why all across Kerry, young men are linin' up to be cared for by meself and me lovely assistant, Miss Bessie-Mae McSorley."

She was rewarded with the ghost of a smile flitting over his face. But it was quickly replaced by a look of worry and one questioning word: "Soldiers?"

"Soldiers!" said Meggy. "Don't be worryin' your poor sore head about soldiers. For, you see, me and some singing Bog Beauties scared them so badly they've likely galloped their poor horses all the way to Dublin, by now." At least, Meggy hoped so. "Ye've nothin' to be worryin' about, except fallin' off Bessie and gainin' a bump on the left to match the one on the right. And that isn't likely to happen, because I've got you trussed up like a hog on market day," joked Meggy, her teasing the only antidote she had for his fear and pain.

Roddy, whose brain was having trouble keeping up, asked, "Bog beauties?"

"Sure, and I'll be tellin' you that tale soon enough. But right now, Bessie and I have you and a treasure to be deliverin' home, and neither man nor beast will be stoppin' us. So close your eyes. I'll be wakin' you with a kiss, when we get there," promised Meggy saucily.

Whether it was the promise or the bump on his head, Roddy quickly nodded off again.

In trying to reassure him, Meggy had cheered herself up as well. After climbing up a bit of a hill and rounding a corner she saw an old hollow tree.

"Could that be the tree where Roddy caught me changin' out of me boy clothes, last summer?" After checking out the area, Meggy smiled, the biggest smile she'd smiled for weeks. Patting Bessie on the rump she said, "Home, girl. We're goin' home."

14

❖

ᴄʜᴇ ᴅᴀɴᴄᴇ ᴏꜰ ʟɪꜰᴇ

They walked on, hearing nothing but the night song of the thrush. Bessie too seemed to know they were close to home and settled into a steady pace. The path was an easy one, worn smooth from the comings and goings of their fellow villagers. Meggy was imagining her homecoming. "I wish we could have arrived earlier. It's so late now, they'll be sound asleep." Picturing the looks on her family's faces when she woke them up made her smile. "I know they won't mind, they'll be haulin' me right into bed with them." That thought made her sigh with a peacefulness she had not felt since leaving Copperkin.

Off in the distance she could see the pub roof. "Roddy, it's your pub. We'll be seein' your da any minute." Bessie started to clip-clop faster. But when they entered the clearing, Meggy suddenly tugged the donkey to a stop.

Something was not right. The pub was dark and silent. No smoke came from its chimney. No laughter came from its doors. Stepping quietly back into the shelter of the woods, Meggy did not know what to think. "Where is everyone? Could it be that it's later than I think?" There was not a voice, not a clue to answer her questions.

The need to go home surged stronger than ever in Meggy. After taking a cautious look around for enemies or soldiers, she headed Bessie and her precious cargo homeward. The path had never seemed so long. Meggy started to feel unexplainable fingers of fear crawl up her back. "The village is so quiet. It feels so empty. What if the soldiers came here, to my home, to my family—when they couldn't find me? What if…" The pictures that visited her mind were too horrible for words, but they held her frozen at the place where the road turned to their cottage. "What if they have torched our cottage? What if Mam and Da and Dan are in prison?"

After all the danger she had faced, she was having trouble gathering up the courage to look at her own home. At last a moan from Roddy got her moving. And there it was, their cottage, just like it had always been—and there was a large candle burning in the window.

Meggy clapped her hands. "It's Christmas Eve. Mam has made the candle to welcome Mary and Joseph. And the door too, will be unlatched." Opening the door she called,

"I'm home! I'm home!" But not a single voice replied. There were no smiles or welcome-home hugs. Meggy felt as empty as the cottage.

She saw that the table was set with bread, milk and another large candle for the Holy Family or any traveler on the road that night. Starving, she had just reached out to tear a chunk off the bread when she heard a moan. "It's selfish I am to be forgettin' Roddy," said Meggy, as she headed out to tend to him. She spoke to him as if he were his usual self. "Now we have a real predicament. I was expectin' Mam, Da and Dan to be here. Mam and I could have you off Bessie's back with as little pain as possible. But I'm not strong enough to get you down and across the room to the settle, without hurting ye."

While she stood figuring out what to do, Bessie-Mae solved the problem. The loyal donkey just walked through the door and right to the bed. She stood there, not so much as twitching an ear, while Meggy untied the ropes that held Roddy onto her back. And then the donkey never budged as her passenger was moved, one painful step at a time, from her back to the bed. Kissing Bessie's shaggy head in gratitude, Meggy said, "You're me hero and the darlingest donkey in all of Ireland."

Bessie raised her head and brayed her agreement, "Aw-ee, aw-ee."

Meggy was surprised to hear a low laugh. It was Roddy, his eyes wide open. "It seems to me that you are gettin' into the habit of kissin' us McSorleys. Do you think one sweet kiss on me head would rid me of the terrible ache I have there?"

Grateful he was returning to his old self, Meggy gave him a kiss without the usual battle. "Are you comfortable, Roddy? Are you warm enough? Would you like a cup of milk?"

Reaching for the pitcher, she saw something she had missed before. It was her Mam's rosary beads curled around a piece of crystal. Fingering them, she suddenly knew where her family was. She showed Roddy. "I think Mam and Dan left this as a message for me. I think it means they are attendin' a secret Christmas Eve mass in our Crystal Cave. I'm going there to fetch Mam and your parents to tend to you. Do you think you'll be all right while I'm gone?"

Roddy, who never wanted her to leave his side again, also felt a deep need for his parents. So he nodded and said, "Bessie will watch over me. But you must come back safe."

Trying not to cry as she turned and left her friend alone, Meggy set her mind to the task at hand. Using a piece of cord, she fashioned a shoulder strap that the sword could hang from. Then she raced off down the path to the Crystal Cave, the sword slapping her pants with every step. The moon and one bright, bright star gave her light. The closer she got, the more the need to see her family grew. She could hardly wait to see the relief in her mother's eyes when she showed her the treasure that would keep them from starvation and homelessness.

Jumping through the sinkhole would have been the fastest way into the Crystal Cave, but Meggy chose the Dragon's Breath Door so as not to disturb the Mass. As she scrambled up the steep rise, someone grabbed her and a deep voice demanded, "Who goes there?"

If not for recognizing the voice, she would have been terrified. But she knew it was a good man, acting as lookout to keep their people safe. "It is me, Mr. McSorley—Meggy."

The strong hold on her arm, turned into a hug as her pulled her to him. "Meggy, Meggy! Thank God you're safe." Looking over her shoulder he was shocked not to see his son. Holding her out away from him he asked, "Where's Roddy? Why isn't he with you?"

Meggy looked into his worried eyes and said, "Your brave son was sorely injured savin' me life. But now he is safe and sound in our settle bed."

Not waiting for any more details, Mr. McSorley escorted her into the tunnel. Meggy stopped in awe at the Dragon's Mouth. The cave was dark and dreary no more. Now it was a magical sanctuary glowing with the light of a hundred candles. Each of the hundred flames cast their brightness in all directions. Meggy gasped. "The cave's crystals are twinklin' as if Fiona's fairies have been up to some Christmas magic."

Distracting her for a moment, Mr. McSorley said, "Roddy's mam will want to be seein' him right away. I'll be takin' her to your cottage, so there is no need for you to hurry back. Stay here with your family and enjoy the mass."

Taking both her hands in his, he said, "We'll always be grateful that you brought our son Roddy back to us." And then he was gone.

Meggy searched each face, lit by the candles they were holding. She saw many she knew, but not the one that she needed to see most. She moved further into the cave. As she wove her way through the gathering of villagers, whispers followed her. "'Tis Meggy, she's home." "Do you think she's earned enough?" "Will she be able to save her family's home?"

The crowd opened up for her, showing the way to her family. Young and old fell quiet as she passed. All watched her with hope in their hearts. When she saw the dear and questioning face of her mother, Meggy nodded once and then ran into her welcoming arms.

All eyes were on the reunion between mother and daughter. Only the dripping of the crystals could be heard as Meggy's mam put one warm and weathered hand on each of her daughter's cold cheeks. She looked at her dear girl's face as if she was trying to burn it into her mind forever.

Meggy hugged Dan tightly to her as he buried his face in her side so the other boys would not see him crying. But her eyes were searching, still searching for her da. "Where is he, where is he, oh, please, let him be here," pleaded Meggy silently. As she searched every candle-lit face again and again, the fear in her grew. She had shoved that fear back every morning and every night for three months. Now it was

swirling up from the bottom of her heart, threatening to drown her. Just when she felt could not take another breath, she felt a strong hand on her shoulder, a strong hand turning her around. Meggy let herself hope the finest of all hopes.

When she looked up, there he was—her da, standing tall, with only a stick to help him. The beam of his smile and the pride in his eyes showed her all was well between them. And then he was struggling to speak, to say the kind of words she thought she might never hear from him again. "Meggy, darling, I'm...so proud—of you. You're...me Christmas—wish—come true."

The light that shone upon Meggy's family seemed to be more than the glow of the candles, more than the glitter of jewels against gold, more even than the loving warmth of their friends and family, gathered there.

Soon Meggy and all those in that light were dancing, dancing with hands clasped and faces smiling, dancing with laughter and with love, dancing the dance of life.

AUTHOR'S NOTE

Like the others in the trilogy, this Meggy tale is set in eighteenth-century Ireland, under the Penal Code. The Penal Code was a set of laws that were extremely unfair to Irish Catholics, forbidding them to educate their children in their own language and religion. Choosing to be a school or dance Master meant living a dangerous life. Masters caught teaching could be fined, beaten, jailed, deported or worse. So classes were taught in secret places and children risked their lives to help their masters escape.

The children faced danger every day, but the beauty of their beloved County Kerry gave them comfort and joy. Even Ireland's placenames are delightful. There are spine tingling ones like Bloody Bridge and Poisoned Glen; fun-to-say names such as Ballinaboola and Drumbohilly; and off course magical-creature names, like Giant's Grave. (I even discovered a place called Fairy Lawn, where a family of Griffins once lived.)

Because these fascinating Irish names were not always where Meggy and I needed them to be, I made up my own. So Meggy's beloved Copperkin exists only in her tales, as do Finfaerie, Drumaderry, Hag's Hollow and Glenmullin.

If you are ever lucky enough to visit Ireland, do not play in the hogweed. The tall hogweed of the Griffins' maze was a harmless native plant of Ireland. Unfortunately nineteenth-century Victorian gardeners planted a tall and toxic non-native hogweed. Holding its hollow stem to your mouth or eyes could result in a serious irritation.

Donkeys like Bessie-Mae were not used in such a way in Ireland until the nineteenth century. Horses carried the creel baskets in which dung was collected. It was definitely used to mend roofs and for fuel, but the dung buns exist only in mine and Roddy's disgusting imaginations.

ACKNOWLEDGEMENTS

Special thanks to artist P. John Burden whose illustrations brought my Meggy and her trilogy of adventures to life.

Thanks to Gary Davies, MSW, Executive Director Brain Injury Association of London and Region who so compassionately shared his expertise about the range of results brain injury patients may experience.